AMA ATA AIDOO has
consultant on education
the English Department c̶ ... ...y ... Ghana, Legon,
where she was immediately appointed Junior Research Fellow of
the Institute of African Studies. Later she was a Fellow of the
Advanced Creative Writing Program at Stanford University and,
in the early 1980s, a Minister of Education in Ghana. While
lecturing in the Department of English at the University of Cape
Coast in the 1970s she was also appointed to serve on the Board
of Directors of the Ghana Broadcasting Corporation, the Arts
Council of Ghana and the Ghana Medical and Dental Council.
She has travelled widely, and has been appointed Visiting
Professor and Distinguished Visiting Professor to the English,
Theatre, African, and African American Studies departments in
a number of universities and colleges in the United States. She is
the Executive Director of Mbaasem, a foundation to support
African women writers and their work.

Her publications include the dramas *The Dilemma of a Ghost*
(Longman, Harlow, 1965) and *Anowa* (Longman, Harlow,
1970); the short stories *No Sweetness Here* (Longman, Harlow,
1970); the novels *Our Sister Killjoy or Reflections from a
Black-Eyed Squint* (Longman, Harlow, 1977) and *Changes*
(The Women's Press, London, 1991); the poetry *Someone
Talking to Sometime* (College Press, Harare, 1985) and *An
Angry Letter in January and Other Poems* (Dangaroo Press,
Coventry, 1992); and the children's books *The Eagle and the
Chickens and Other Stories* (Tana Press, Enugu, 1986) and
Birds and Other Poems (College Press, Harare, 1987).

Ama Ata Aidoo's many awards include the Nelson Mandela
Prize for Poetry in 1987 for *Someone Talking to Sometime* and
the Commonwealth Writers' Prize for Africa for *Changes* in
1992.

AMA ATA AIDOO has distinguished herself as a writer and as a commentator on education and gender issues. She graduated from the English Department of the University of Ghana, Legon, where she was immediately appointed Junior Research Fellow of the Institute of African Studies. Later she was a fellow of the Advanced Creative Writing Program at Stanford University and in the early 1970s, a Lecturer of Education in Ghana. While teaching in the Department of English at the University of Cape Coast in the 1970s, she was also appointed a member of the Board of Directors of the Ghana Broadcasting Corporation, the Arts Council of Ghana, and the Ghana Medical and Dental Council. She has travelled widely, and has often appointed Visiting Professor and Distinguished Visiting Professor in English, Theatre, African, and African American Studies departments in a number of universities and colleges in the United States. She is the Executive Director of Mbaasem, a foundation to support African women writers and their work.

Her publications include the dramas The Dilemma of a Ghost (1965) and Anowa (1970), the short stories No Sweetness Here (1970); the novels Our Sister Killjoy or Reflections from a Black-Eyed Squint (Harlow, 1977) and Changes (The Women's Press, London, 1991); the poetry collections Someone Talking to Sometime (1985) and An Angry Letter in January and Other Poems (Dangaroo Press, Coventry, 1992); and the children's books The Eagle and the Chickens and Other Stories (1986) and Birds and Other Poems (College Press, Harare, 1987).

Ama Ata Aidoo's many awards include the Nelson Mandela Prize for Poetry in 1987. Her novel Changes: a Love Story won the Commonwealth Writers' Prize for Africa (Best Book) in 1992.

AMA ATA AIDOO

THE GIRL WHO CAN
AND OTHER STORIES

Heinemann

Heinemann is an imprint of Pearson Education Limited, a
company incorporated in England and Wales, having its registered
office at Edinburgh Gate, Harlow, Essex, Cm20 2JE.
Registered company number: 872828

www.heinemann.co.uk

Heinemann is a registered trademark of Pearson Education Limited

First published by Sub-Saharan Publishers in 1997

British Library Cataloguing in Publication Data
A catalogue record for this book is available from the British Library.

Phototypeset by SetSystems Ltd, Saffron Walden, Essex

Printed by Multivista Global Ltd.

ISBN 978 0 435 91013 6

11 12 13 14 / 10 9 8 7

Acknowledgements
A number of the stories were published individually for the first time in the
following journals, magazines and anthologies. In every instance, it was
with the understanding that the author remained the copyright holder.
'She Who Would be King' - *A Rising Public Voice, Women in Politics
Worldwide*, The Feminist Press, New York, USA, 1995; 'Heavy Moments' -
Soho Square, Bloomsbury Publishing, London, England, 1992; 'Lice' -
published for the first time as 'Loos' in a Swedish translation, in *Rapport*,
the in-house magazine of SIDA, Goteburg, May, 1986 and for the first time
in English in *West Africa*, London, England, March 1987; 'The Girl Who
Can' - MS Magazine, New York March 1985; 'Male-ing Names in the
Sun' - *Unbecoming Daughters of the Empire*, Dangaroo Press, Aarhaus,
Denmark, 1992; 'Nowhere Cool' - *Asemka*, a journal of the University of
Cape Coast, Ghana, 1974. This completely restructured version first
appeared in *Callaloo*, Johns Hopkins University, 1990; 'Payments' -
originally published as 'Satisfaction?' in the English Department's
Departmental Work-papers, University of Cape Coast, Ghana, 1971.

For
Barbara Bowman:
who cautioned and then nurtured;

Ayi Kwei Armah and Alice Walker
– at the very least, in kinship reciprocity;

and some of the girls who can:

Kinna Likimani, Belinda Lartey, Gifty Abban, Grace Enapanyin
Acheampong, Adwoa Serwaa Acheampong, Efua Entsifua
Aidoo, Yvonne Aba Barden, Nana Ama Barnes, Ekua Barbara
Brown, J. Abra Degbor, Angela Leila Lwindi Hassan, Mumbi
Mugo, Njeri Mugo, Priya Narayanan, Nana Tia Nikoi, Faith
Kasire Nsereko, Indira Odamtten, Adwoa Fosuwa Ayisi-
Okyere, Adwoa Mansa Ayisi-Okyere, Nana Osafo-Gyimah,
Nana Ekua Osei, Efua Oteng-Adjei, Pamela Waterman, Rachel
Nana Gyesiwa Watts, Efua Anowa Wilson-Tagoe . . .

CONTENTS

Her Hair Politics

– a very short story

'It's not easy.'

She was superb. The words rolled off her tongue like pips from oranges or cherries: articles thrown away with wistful abandon, to be forgotten utterly or later, maybe, searched for, and used.

She was great: an advocate who could stand her ground with the best of them. A lawyer who knew how to get all to see her point. Their lordships would have been wowed.

The piece, she swore, would keep its shape, its texture, for years and years and years. 'Pliant and pliable, you can plait, perm and pleat, roll it up in a bun, flatten for the early twentieth century look, or just curl it up for a Louis Quatorze.' Oh yes. She knew them all: the monarchs of Europe, and their wives and mistresses, who had given their names to coiffures.

'It's not at all easy.'

She promised me a new look. The piece, she vowed, would change my life. For the better of course: give me a kind of beauty beyond my wildest dreams. I had declined in the only way I knew how, pleaded my perennial poverty, other commitments that demanded cash, the children's school fees and the one thousand extras that caused sources and resources to haemorrhage heavier, and faster, than Vic Falls.

'Madame, it is real human hair,' she had said.

'Is it?' I'd asked. I could already feel the giant weals rising on my back, around my neck, over my bosom.

'Yes, it is. Feel it. It is so soft.'

1

'No,' I'd declined, my voice low, and softer than her precious merchandise.

I did not tell her I was getting ready to be sick.

A mop of silky hair: lovingly grown, diligently fed, nursed, and pampered to yield its best in brilliant black sheen that breathes and glows like a sated mamba, then cut, and sold? For just feelgood resource for shoes and hats and jewellery? Or, most likely because there must be rice, clothes for mother's back, something to hide in case of sickness or death? . . .

'Somebody else's burden?' I'd asked. 'No thank you.'

Then she lost her song, her cool. She stared at me, not knowing what on earth I was talking about, but very clear only that she had lost her custom, her cause, her case. She started to cry, while I went away to vomit . . .

. . . wondering where such unease could well up from, and wondering who I thought I was, who could sneer at my sisters' lifeline, spitting on people from the Pacific to the Atlantic and back again? Sure, her hair had been handled many times, if not by a hundred pairs of hands, and those hands were attached to mouths that must be fed, and all those mouths could, maybe, eat a little because she grew her hair.

And so my Sister, that's how I came to weep for us all.

'No, it's not easy.'

2

Choosing

– a moral from the world of work

Once upon a time, there was a writer who couldn't write because she thought she had too many problems. The main one being financial. So one day, she decided she would go and do other things from which she could make money more quickly. That way, she would be able to solve her problems, since half of them had to do with the fact that she never had enough money to solve her problems. To begin with, she decided to be a teacher.

'Yes,' she said to herself, 'I care a great deal about young growing minds. And in any case, at the end of every month I would be paid something for the job I would do.'

So The Writer went into teaching. And she loved it. She was very happy because she had always felt that of all the work that anybody can do in this world, teaching is one of the best jobs. And for a while, everything was fine. She was a good teacher too. The children liked her classes. She made everything she taught sound as if it had something to do with the lives they lived in their homes, as well as the lives they would live one day, when they grew up. She also made them laugh about life; being young, growing up and grown-ups. One thing the children noticed was that the way she taught them made things so much easier to learn.

Indeed, everything should have ended happily ever after for The Writer-Turned-Teacher. But it didn't. She was having some completely new problems. One was that just before she took the

3

teaching job, she had begun to write a book which she had hoped to continue working on in her spare time. However, after some time, it occurred to her that she was not working on her book. It had turned out that teaching was not just a matter of standing in front of children to talk. She had to prepare what she planned to teach. She had to do the actual teaching. She had to set her classes some work to do in school or for homework. She had to mark the work the classes turned in, and then prepare some more work to teach. Then back to the actual teaching, and on and on and on.

Then she found something about herself at the end of each school day. She was very happy, but she was also very tired. In fact, she was so happy and so tired that she did not want to sit down and write a book. All she wanted to do was to have a bath, or a shower, or go to the sea and swim. After that she wanted to drink some fresh orange juice or a cup of tea or even a bowl of soup. Then she wanted to cook and feed herself, after which she wanted to visit her mother, or a friend, or sit down and listen to some good music: on her player, or her tape recorder, or in the night club near where she lived, or live, as played by a new group in her neighbourhood. And then after that just to lie down and sleep . . .

So for a long time, The Writer-Turned-Teacher did not add even a single word to her book. And soon, that began to worry her. She would remember her book the last thing before she drifted off to sleep, and the first thing as soon as she woke up. And her heart always jumped with sadness when this happened.

After a while, The Writer-Turned-Teacher began to think about her book even when she was at school and in front of her classes. She would be talking and, in the middle of a sentence, forget what she was saying and just stare into space. At first, it happened only once in a while: and when she caught herself

4

doing it, she covered up quickly so her classes wouldn't notice. But things got worse. She began to forget herself for longer times, and more often. So, very soon, her pupils could not help but notice. And unlike grown-ups who can notice bad things around them or about themselves, or other people, and can pretend or must pretend they don't see, the children in the classes of The Writer-Turned-Teacher would not pretend. First they wondered, each to himself or herself, about what was happening to their teacher. Then they began to laugh and giggle, until one day, she also began to notice their behaviour. That evening, she went home and sat down to do some thinking. But doing all the thinking by herself, she got into some serious muddle. Things were going round and round in her head.

Then she remembered a proverb her mother had told her once: 'One head cannot form a council,' which means that it is not easy to hold a meeting with yourself and come out with a proper decision. So she got up and went to see her mother who, although she had never been to school at all, seemed to know quite a few things about this life and how it can be lived.

When The Writer-Turned-Teacher went to her mother, The Mother asked her to sit down. She did. They started by discussing a few things that a mother anywhere would discuss with a daughter. After some time, The Mother said:

'Ah my daughter, I know you. It was not really to talk about these matters that you came. There is something else. What is it?'

The Writer-Turned-Teacher told her mother all that had been happening: about deciding to go and teach, and not writing her book.

'I see you have a problem,' said The Mother. 'But every problem can be solved. Sometimes not in the way we would want. But then we have to take a little of something we don't want once in a while ... You say that you like teaching; but

5

these days, you are thinking of your book so much that you are not teaching well?'

'Yes, Mother,' replied The Writer-Turned-Teacher, very sadly.

'Well,' said The Mother, 'that is not good enough . . . So why don't you stop teaching, and go back to writing your book?'

'But I like the teaching work,' answered The Writer, 'and I need the money.'

'Hmm,' The Mother sighed heavily. She was thinking that her daughter was in trouble. Very big trouble.

'Now, now, now,' she said aloud, but not too unkindly, 'let us take one thing at a time. First the money business. Ahhh,' The Mother spoke almost to herself: 'Money, money . . . it is bad . . . if only because it has to come into everything?' Then again aloud, she asked her daughter: 'But why must you go and teach to earn money if writing is what you like most to do?'

The Writer-Turned-Teacher couldn't believe her ears. Why was her mother pretending as if she did not know her troubles? She was almost angry. But then she remembered something else her mother had told her at some other time now long past: 'You cannot allow yourself to be angry in a discussion out of which you hope to get something good.'

So she quickly shut the door to her anger, and calmly told her mother that she really liked teaching. Almost as much as she liked writing. But with writing, she always had to wait for a long time before a story or a book brought in money. And even when the money came, it was so little, it was never good for much . . .

'Mother,' she continued, 'although I hope that one day the money from my books would be enough to take care of my problems, that day seems to be very, very far off.'

'Well, why don't you borrow? Since one day you may be able to pay back what you borrow today?' The Mother suggested.

'But Mother, *you* have told me that we should not borrow from friends. Because that sort of thing spoils friendships . . . and in the meantime you "(I) have no money to give me (you)".'

The Mother also spoke to agree with her, and both of them finished at the same time.

'I know, I know,' The Mother said, 'I wish I had more than my love and understanding to give you.'

After she said that The Writer jumped up, and went to hug her mother.

'Ah, Mother,' she said, 'thank you. Some people don't even get love and understanding from anybody. Don't worry, I shall think of something.'

'How about going to the bank?' was The Mother's next suggestion.

'I have gone there over and over and over again,' The Writer said. 'But you see, they won't give me a loan.'

'Why not?' asked The Mother.

'Because they say that although everybody enjoys the things writers write, they (the banks) don't like lending money to writers to live on and write.'

'But why?' The Mother was really shocked.

'Because they say that banks deal with things that are secure, and with people who deal with things that are secure. Like investing in business: manufacturing and commerce. But then, writers deal with books and there is no security in books.'

'Why not?' The Mother asked.

'Mother,' The Writer began to reply, trying hard not to let her irritation return, 'they point out that after a writer has written a book, no one, not even the writer, knows for sure that a publisher would publish it. And if a publisher took it and published it, no one knows for sure that the bookshops would take them wholesale to sell . . . And if the booksellers took them, they cannot be sure that people would buy them to read!'

The Mother was nodding her head with growing understanding.

'So you see,' The Writer added, 'they don't give us loans because no one knows for sure that any book a writer writes will ever make money. If we had precious things that did not move, like money, and jewels, and houses, and land itself, they would take them as "security" against which they could loan us money to live on and write. But very few writers have money that does not move, or jewels, houses and land. And I am not one of them.'

'But my dear daughter, why would anyone who already had money and jewels and houses and land want to go borrow money from the bank? ... and why should the banks lend money to such people?'

The Writer-Turned-Teacher wanted to tell her mother that indeed in this world, people who have money always want to borrow some more. And it was also exactly people like that who got money from the banks without trouble. But she did not say it. Because it would take them too far from what they were discussing. And in any case, she was sure her mother knew all that already, never mind what she was pretending to know or not to know, for the sake of the discussion.

'Mother,' she continued, 'the bankers say that giving a loan to a writer to live on and write a book is a gamble. And they are not gamblers. They are serious business people. What shall I do, Mother?'

'Hmm, it's very difficult,' said The Mother. 'But please, answer one question for me . . . You say you like teaching?'

'Yes, Mother. The children made me feel good when they showed understanding for what I was trying to teach. And being with them . . .' The Writer-Turned-Teacher was going to go into details. But her mother cut her short.

'I hear you, I hear you. You like teaching very much. Yet

8

recently, you have been thinking of how your work on the book has stopped?'

'Yes, Mother.'

'Even in the classroom?'

'Yes, Mother.'

'Then please, answer this one question for me . . .' The Mother said, forgetting that she had said the same thing before asking her daughter at least one other question earlier. But The Writer knew her mother was leading her on to a real big question. So instead of getting impatient, she waited, alert for whatever was coming next. 'My daughter, did you also think of teaching or worry about not doing some other job when you were writing?'

'No,' The Writer-Turned-Teacher answered quickly and simply, but also with surprise at the way her mother's mind worked. 'When I am writing, I don't even remember that any other kind of work exists that human beings ought to do.'

'Ah,' said her mother with appreciation. 'I thought so.'

The discussion had come to a junction where The Writer felt she did not know where to turn or whether to turn at all. On the other hand, The Mother was thinking that they had come to a point beyond which she could not go with her daughter. Her daughter had to continue the rest of the journey herself.

'Mother,' said The Writer-Turned-Teacher, 'what shall I do?'

'My daughter,' The Mother was very quick with her reply. 'Frankly, I don't know,' she said, 'I can only discuss your problems with you. This may help to make things a little clearer for you, since no single head can hold a conference. But when it comes to making a decision, you have to do that for yourself.'

The Writer understood. Although, deep down in her heart, she was also wishing that apart from giving birth to children, and looking after the children while they grew up, and (sometimes) giving up their time to discuss things with their children even when they were grown up, mothers also made decisions for their children. Then, she felt ashamed for thinking such a cowardly thought. What she did not know was that almost everybody in this world who has a mother thinks like that at some time or other. Especially when they are faced with a difficult decision: which is also when orphans miss their mothers most, never mind how old they are . . . At long last, The Writer-Turned-Teacher said: 'Mother, I know what I must do.'

'Yes?' asked her mother eagerly.

'I think I am going to stop teaching,' The Writer announced.

'And do what?' her mother asked, with her eyes shining. So great was her excitement.

'You see,' said The Writer, 'although I liked teaching very much, I put too much of myself into it. I did not have time or even the mind for my writing. So in the end, I only worried: and that spoilt the teaching work too. Besides, teaching is really like writing. They don't pay much for it in this country, and the money was really not enough for all the things I needed money to do. The only difference was that the money from teaching came regularly.'

'So what are you going to do?' The Mother cut in.

'I'm going into trading. I'm going to buy and sell.'

Her mother was shocked. 'Y-E-S?' she asked her daughter.

'Mother,' the daughter was very quick with her answer, 'trading would be the kind of work that should give me enough money quickly to take care of my problems and leave me with some time to write.'

'Y-E-S?' The Mother was not even trying to get convinced.

'Yes, Mother, yes,' The Writer was very sure, 'you and I know of people who make in one day of buy-and-sell all that I made in over six months of teaching. Or in the last five years from my writing,' she reminded her mother.

'Yes?' asked her mother again. 'I think you should think this particular decision over very carefully,' she finally suggested.

'Yes . . .' once again came the strong clear voice of the daughter: almost as if she had not really heard what her mother had just said. 'And because unlike teaching, trading would be very, very different from writing, even if I felt good and got tired doing it, it would be a different goodness and a different tiredness. It could not possibly take away my desire to write at the end of the day.'

The Mother was not at all impressed.

'And think of it, Mother,' The Writer-Turned-Teacher-and-at-the-Crossroads was not giving up convincing herself.

'Besides,' she said, 'because no one would be paying me to work, I shall control my time better . . . Oh, it's perfect, Mother. It is absolutely perfect.'

She had been getting more and more excited as she spoke. Now she stood up, and started dancing and jumping all over the place. She thought she had found the perfect solution to all her problems. However, it was clear her mother was not at all happy about the way things were turning out. She was tempted to tell her daughter that she was making a terrible mistake. But she told herself that she had to leave her daughter to try things out, and especially go out there and discover about herself and the world she lived in. It was not a very easy decision for The Mother to make. But in the end she made it, and wished her daughter well. Then they parted, the daughter promising to drop by to see her mother, once in a while, as she had been doing all her grown-up life. The Mother, like all mothers, prayed in her heart for her daughter, that things would go well in spite of her not being sure about the wisdom in her daughter's newest plans.

After returning to her own home from her mother's, The Writer-Turned-Teacher-Now-Considering-Trading did not waste

11

time. She went round looking for money to put into her new scheme. She had a little money of her own, just about the sum of her last pay from teaching. And that was not enough to start a serious trading business with. She needed real money. Luckily for her, when she went to the bank, things turned out to be much easier for her, now that she wanted a loan to trade with. Her Bank Manager smiled, rubbed his hands and told her that the bank had a policy to help beginners like her. 'Nothing big, you understand. Er ... er ... Miss er ... er ... but there is something. It is our policy at the 5th World Century Trust to encourage entrepreneurship in the general population ... Especially young women.' He winked at The Writer-Turned-Teacher-Now-Becoming-a-Trader.

He pulled out a gold-looking cigarette case, took out a cigarette, knocked the end where cigarettes are normally lighted on the gold-looking case in order to be sure that all the loose tobacco stayed inside the cigarette. He then lighted it and began to smoke. He pulled out some papers from a drawer, pushed them toward the Writer and asked her to please fill them. With his friendly advice and hints, The Writer-Turned-Teacher-Turning-into-a-Trader soon filled the papers. The Bank Manager took them back, told her he would see to it that they were processed as quickly as possible, shook hands with her, and asked her to come back after a day or two. After two days, The Writer-Turned-Teacher-Turning-into-a-Trader went back to the bank, and sure enough, the loan was ready. She collected the money, laughing all the way home.

So now The Writer could set about organizing her new business. She went around buying goods to sell: dresses for young women and children, shirts for all ages, beads and mirrors. Also around this time, she looked for a stall to rent in the city market. She thought she had to be where other people who sold her type

12

of goods were. But then a cousin who knew a little more about such things told her that it was the wrong thing to do.

'Those stalls are for the traders who are more settled,' the cousin said.

'So where should I sell?' The Writer-Turned-Teacher-Turned-Trader asked. 'No problem,' the cousin quickly replied. 'Go to the market gates. Look for one of the busiest, and put your table there. Spread your goods and call out with your bell. Things would be more brisk for you.' What the cousin was saying seemed to make a lot of sense. After all, anyone who wanted to do any marketing had to pass through one of the market gates.

'But how about the market wardens?' The Writer asked her cousin, as she remembered there could be problems with hawking wares.

'What about them?' her cousin asked back.

'Well ... you see ...' began the writer, sounding rather unsure of herself for the first time since she had decided to go into trading.

'You see, the market wardens are always chasing hawkers away from the gates, and when the hawkers are caught, they are fined rather heavily, no?'

'My dear, if you are going to be so timid, how can you go into trading? Of course, the market wardens chase away the hawkers from the market gates. But didn't you say "always"?'

'Yes,' The Writer-Turned-Teacher-Turned-Trader answered, even more timidly, and wondering what her cousin was driving at.

'Well,' her cousin said, 'that shows that even if they always get chased away or get heavily fined, they also always return there. Maybe because they know from experience that they do quite well at the gates: getting chased, getting fined and all.' It was half an advice and half a scolding.

13

So The Writer-Turned-Teacher-Turned-Trader thanked her cousin and dropped the idea of getting a proper stall. Instead, she purchased a second-hand table and a small hawker's bell. And the very next day, she took her stuff to the market gates. The gate she had selected was the main gate, the biggest gate and also the first gate that was built during the construction of the market. In fact, whereas the other gates had names like East Gate, or Gate of the Yams, that gate was known to everybody simply as 'The Gate'.

That first morning, The Writer-Turned-Teacher-Turned-Trader left home quite early like any other trader. She went straight to The Gate. She spread her goods out just when others were spreading out theirs. It was all such capital fun, she thought. An incredibly colourful life so different from the life she had known.

'What fun ... what fun ... what fun!' she couldn't help exclaiming. She truly loved being in the middle of the hustle and bustle at The Gate. She was with people and life. Soon, she even remembered some of her non-writing friends who had always told her to leave her desk because writing was a bourgeois, self-serving and snobbish job. 'Don't sit in a room writing about life. Get up, get out and live it.' They always teased her. So as she rang her bell and reached out to the people passing by in an effort to get them to come and look at her wares, she wished those friends would see her now. She was out there mingling and struggling with life. Real life ...

One or two people stopped by her goods to look at this or that. At the beginning, they always moved on. Then they began to stop. One ... Two ... Three. Soon, it was a small crowd. Clearly, a lot of people were finding both her goods and her prices quite attractive. She was pleased. Very, very pleased. Of course, the market wardens came to chase her and the other traders away. She learnt from the others and quickly regrouped.

She soon met some other big problem though. And that big problem was herself. It was becoming very clear even during that first week that maybe she did not know how to sell much of anything to anybody. To begin with, she could not make herself stick to her prices, although she had taken time to work out the cost of the items and decided on a price to sell each of them, at which she could recover the loan, and make a profit. However, once she was actually at the market and her stuff was all nicely arranged at The Gate, she behaved as if the person who fixed the prices for the goods and the one who sold them were two different people. Even before someone had asked the price of a shirt or a dress, she found herself getting ready to quote a lower price. Of course, most people love bargains. So no matter how low she quoted the prices, the buyers always asked for even lower figures. And most of the time, she gave in to them, especially when she thought a buyer was quite poor. In fact, quite often, by the time she was paid for something, she had sold it for far less than the price she had bought it for: sometimes by as much as half the price lower. Very soon, most of the people who came to buy from The Gate stopped by her table without hesitating for a moment. People like getting things cheaply, especially good things.

It was not long before other sellers at The Gate began to feel jealous and murmur about The Writer-Turned-Teacher-Turned-Trader.

'What does she think she is doing?' asked one.

'I know what she is doing,' another quickly answered. 'She is taking away all our customers. That's what she is doing.'

'But we can't let her. She is just a newcomer.'

'She is a writer. She should stick to writing.'

'She is a woman.'

'She is a stranger.'

'She is a foreigner!'

A third, a fourth and a fifth joined in. At that point, the third person suggested that they go and throw her and her goods out. They nearly rushed on her. But the first speaker who was herself a woman stopped them. She suggested that with their permission, she would go and talk to The Writer-Turned-Teacher-Turned-Trader about the way she should behave at The Gate. After which they should give her another day or two. If things did not change, then they could throw her out. The others were not too happy with the suggestion. But they agreed to it for the meantime.

What the other traders at The Gate didn't know was that although The Writer-Turned-Teacher-Turned-Trader was pulling the crowds all right, she was not really selling much, and what she sold was always at a loss. She had said that she was going into trading to make money quickly to solve her problems and have time to write. But then, she did not have what all good economists describe as the profit motive, and in trading the profit motive is very important. It is the grand way of describing what makes other people strong-headed and hard-hearted enough to sell things to others at prices that are well above what they know the things are worth.

The Writer-Turned-Teacher-Turned-Trader herself did not know that she didn't have the profit motive. But her mother, her friends, her close and distant relatives, and all the people who knew her well had long ago suspected that she did not have it. And very early in her trading, her customers too learned that about her.

There were other things The Writer-Turned-Teacher-Turned-Trader was doing which were also not at all good for trading. For instance, when people came to her table to ask about her goods, she spent too much time talking to them about how she got the goods, and where. Then in turn, some of the buyers would tell her their hardship stories. How they had a cousin's

16

brother's wife's sister in hospital. Or how they had lost their father recently. Or how they had just been burgled. And The Writer-Turned-Teacher-Turned-Trader would stop minding her goods and stand listening to the stories. Of course, there is something in every writer that also likes to listen to stories. So she listened. And most of the time, she was moved by the sad tales she heard. In fact, she was often so moved that she would give an item like a shirt away to the speaker for free. Sometimes, she also gave things on credit to people who never came back to pay her.

Meanwhile, some of the buyers were in fact not buyers at all but tsotsis who wanted to come and see if they could steal some of her stuff. They were a mixed group of young men and a few young women. Some stole because they really were poor and had no jobs. They needed the things they stole – like shirts to wear and dresses to sell for the cash. There were others who stole because they were young, with plenty of energy which no one had helped them to make good use of. So now they were bored, and stealing and generally harassing people like The Writer-Turned-Teacher-Turned-Trader was just something to do to kill time. Anyway, the tsotsis quickly marked out The Writer-Turned-Teacher-Turned-Trader as someone who was excellent for them to go to. They would divide themselves into about three groups. When they got to her table, one or two of them pretended to be seriously asking her for her prices. Another one or two – usually younger – started telling her very sad stories which never failed to get her attention; then the third lot began to snatch away shirts, dresses, babies' clothes and anything else they fancied. They gave these things to the last group who hovered in the background just to receive them. Therefore, between what the tsotsis took; what she herself gave away to real and pretending poor people; what people bought on credit and never came back to pay for; and the cash she lost from too

17

much low pricing, The Writer-Turned-Teacher-Turned-Trader was not only making no profit, but in fact she was losing a great deal of money each day.

So how could the other sellers at The Gate still have been angry with her if they had known what was going on?

Meanwhile, all the time she was busy trading, The Writer-Turned-Teacher-Turned-Trader was not writing much. In fact, when she could be honest with herself, she admitted she was writing nothing. She had no time. This was because her days were divided into those she spent going around buying the goods, and those she spent at The Gate selling. In the evening, she found herself counting, calculating and trying to balance her accounts: of what she had bought and for how much; what she had sold and for how much; how much goods were left and how much money she had in her purse. This very often took her late into the night. But then, her accounts never balanced up, no matter how late she stayed up. And it was easy to see why. She was not a good accountant. She had neither been born with a gift for accounting, nor had been trained as an accountant.

One day, she even went out and bought a calculator. But then, that did not help her much. Because a calculator can only add up figures that are fed into it in the first place. It cannot work with figures that don't exist: for instance, of clothes and other items pinched by thieves or things given away in sympathy as gifts to people one correctly or mistakenly considered to be poor. Therefore, most evenings, The Writer-Turned-Teacher-Turned-Trader just stopped counting and calculating and went to bed late at night or in the small hours of the morning. Not really because her figures made sense even to herself. She was just tired. So at what time was she ever going to write?

In any case, it could not go on forever. One day, The Writer-Turned-Trader went back home to The Gate, checked on her stocks, and discovered that all her goods were gone. Yet she did not have a single penny, or pesewa or cent or kobo or thebe or peso or whatever, in her purse. She had lost what little she herself had had, as well as what the bank had loaned her.

That night, The Writer-Turned-Teacher-Turned-Trader did not sleep at all. Not that she didn't want to. She couldn't. She sat and wondered what to do. Morning came and still she didn't know. As she saw the morning sun, she remembered that she still had a mother. So she decided to go and see her, although she also felt a little ashamed about letting her mother know that her buying and selling trade had collapsed. But she also remembered that mothers are sometimes like pillows; when everything fails, you can cry on them. And never for the smallest bit of time that night did she remember that she had a book to write.

This time, when she got to her mother's house, The Writer-Turned-Teacher-Turned-Trader did not pretend that she had just gone to say 'hello' to her mother. She did not even sit down properly before starting on her story. She told her mother everything: about where she had thought she could go and sell from; about the cousin's advice; about her life at The Gate: the thieves, the unfriendliness of the other traders, her losses. Everything; everything. As for The Mother, she listened carefully to the story and never even once interrupted her daughter.

The Writer had told herself that she was going to be very brave and not cry. So telling the story, she had not cried. She had only shown a great excitement. But normally, or maybe only sometimes, and luckily, mothers actually know better. So after she had finished telling her story, her mother pulled her into her arms, and rocked her like she had done when The Writer was a baby. It made The Writer-Turned-Teacher-Turned-Trader feel good. She was comforted. However, because she was not a baby anymore, she could not allow herself to fall asleep in her mother's arms. So after a while, she pulled herself up, and asked her mother what she thought had gone wrong. The Mother spoke at last, and this is what she said:

'My daughter, do you remember the day we discussed what you could do after you left teaching?'

'Yes Mother,' The Writer replied.

'And you told me you were going into trading because you should make more money anyway ... to take care of your problems and leave you time to write?'

'Yes, Mother,' said The Writer.

'Well?' asked The Mother.

'But why did it not go right, Mother?' The Writer asked. She was beginning to get excited again.

'Actually, I really didn't think it sounded right,' The Mother said calmly.

'What do you mean, Mother? Why didn't you think it sounded right?' The Writer's voice was now like the voice of someone who was angrily beginning not to believe her ears. Her mother was very calm.

'I thought it was not what you should do,' she said quietly.

'W – h – a – t?' The Writer exploded.

'Yes, my dear daughter,' The Mother was very sure. 'In fact, I had always known that you could never sell a thing to anybody.'

For a while, The Writer appeared to be too angry and too hurt to open her mouth and speak. She could not understand it. How could her own mother keep such knowledge from her? How could her own mother not want to help her? How could her own mother betray her so? But The Mother just sat, and watched, and waited for what her daughter would say or do next. She knew that her daughter was suffering very badly. She also knew that sometimes, people have to do their own suffering. All anyone who loves them can do is show that they care. After some time, the daughter asked her mother with pretended calm:

'But Mother, if you knew that I was wrong, and that trading was not the right thing for me, why didn't you warn me? Why didn't you prevent me from going into buy-and-sell? . . . Why, Mother, why?'

For the first time since the beginning of the discussion, The Mother smiled.

'Calm down, and listen,' she said. 'I did not try to prevent you going into buying and selling because I was in the discussion only to help you make up your mind. Therefore the only thing I could do once you had made your decision was for me to make sure that that was the decision you really wanted to make. You see?'

'Yes, Mother,' the daughter replied, although her mother had not even expected her to reply. The daughter was seeing and not quite seeing.

'And definitely,' The Mother continued, 'that day you appeared to be very sure . . .'

'So sure that in fact, you were (I was) busy dancing up and down.' They had spoken together again. But this time, The Writer had continued when her mother stopped. 'But Mother,' she insisted, 'you could still have said something . . . Yes. And you could have done something.'

The Mother could feel herself getting a little angry with her daughter, but she killed the anger even before it could be born. 'Oh yes, I suppose I could still have done something . . .' she said in her quiet way, almost to herself.

'So why didn't you?' The Writer was angry now, and her voice sounded as if she was now openly accusing her mother of something like betrayal; an absence of concern and love. The Mother sat up, stretched a little and then said, 'My daughter, you see, anything I said or did then would have been useless or even dangerous. I would have prevented you from working things out for yourself. I would have been interfering in your affairs . . . What could I have said? That I knew you would fail as a trader? . . . And do you know what would have happened after I had said that?'

The daughter shook her head.

'One of two things,' The Mother continued. 'You could have been angry with me for not showing confidence in you; and then ignored me and gone into buying and selling anyway, while feeling bad about having defied me. So that when things didn't work out, you wouldn't have had the courage to come to see me . . .'

The Writer could only nod her head with growing understanding.

'On the other hand,' The Mother continued, 'if you had succeeded after I had warned you about the possibility of failure, you would still have felt bad about having managed to do well without listening to me . . . But that feeling would have been mixed with another one. You would have been glad that I had been proved wrong . . . And from then on, both you and I would have felt that I was just an old fool after all, whose ideas you need not ever again bother with. You would have had an even better excuse not to want to discuss your problems with me after that.' The Mother's voice was beginning to sound a little sad.

'But I may not have disobeyed you,' declared The Writer. 'I might have listened to you and not gone into trading at all.' The daughter thought she had to remind her mother that there was another possibility. That she could have been an obedient child.

'A – h – h – h, exactly,' The Mother sighed heavily. 'That was the other thing I feared. Your obedience. In fact I feared that most.'

'Why?'

'Because that too could have created the same problem, although in a different way.'

'How?' The Writer asked.

22

'You see,' continued The Mother, 'I am not rich. So I could not have given you money to help solve your problems. And until you found a good and lasting solution to your financial problems, you would always have wondered if you had not made a mistake listening to my advice against you going into trading. And when things got really bad, you would have blamed me deep in your heart. And this too would have stopped you from ever coming to me (you) with your (my) problems ever again.' The daughter joined her mother, and the two finished speaking together.

'Oh Mother,' the daughter protested. But she was beginning to understand what her mother was trying to say, and she was also beginning to feel better.

'So are you saying, Mother, that whatever you did, you could have lost me? Apart from the course you took?'

'Yes,' said The Mother.

'And you did not want to lose me?' The Writer's voice was showing relief and pleasure all at once.

'Of course not. I mean, yes. Or no . . . whatever . . . I don't want to lose you . . . What an idea!' The Mother and The Writer were laughing and hugging.

After a while, The Mother said, 'But listen, there is an even more important reason why I didn't insist that you did things my way . . .'

'You mean more important than your fear of losing me?' The Writer asked. She was very surprised. She was also scared. Because however old we get, we don't want to hear – ever – that our mothers would not mind losing us in the hope of gaining something else!! What could that thing be? And how big could it be?

'Yes,' The Mother said.

'Aha?' The Writer was not keen to hear what that reason was.

The Mother paused to choose her words carefully:

'You see, we do not bring children into this world to solve their problems for them. That would be useless and dangerous. For one, it helps no one at all. Besides, if we keep doing that, very soon, our children would have no problems at all to solve. They would become too stupid to even have problems. And believe this, my daughter, a life without problems is no life at all!!!'

The Writer just sat, watching her mother and thinking about what her mother had just said. Then she knew her mother was completely right.

'So, Mother, now I am back to where I was?' she asked.

'Not at all,' said her mother.

'But . . .' The Writer began again.

'But nothing,' said The Mother, cutting her daughter short without feeling bad. 'How can you say you are back to where you had started? That is not possible. Try to think of what you have gone through, and how far you have travelled.'

'But I still don't have the money to solve my problems, and I still have not written my book.'

The Mother strongly disagreed with her.

'It is true that you still don't have the money to solve your problems and you still haven't written your book. But that does not mean you are where you were. Indeed, you are very far ahead. You have learnt something about yourself and the world, no? Of course, if we are talking of money, then true-true, you are very far back, since you have lost the little money you had, as well as what you borrowed from the bank! So one way you have gone backwards, and another way you are forward. But neither way are you where you were.'

'Mother, what can I do?' The Writer's voice was beginning to show the old panic.

'It seems to me that the only way out would be to do best, what you do well,' her mother said.

'But Mother, writing is what I do well and already do – best. But writing does not pay! ... And will not pay however well I do it!' The Writer screamed.

'Well, find a way to make it pay,' The Mother said simply. However, from her voice, you could guess that the older woman was thinking that the discussion had gone on too long, and she was wishing it was over. The Writer turned to look at her mother as if the older person had suddenly gone mad.

'Well ... Well ...' The Mother stammered ... 'Well ... maybe that is not what you want to hear. Or in fact, what I should be telling you. But young woman, you know that you have tried; and now you also know some of the things you cannot do to solve your problems.'

'In fact, buying and selling has created more problems for me,' The Writer herself added. 'You see?' said The Mother. 'In this life, there can only be two ways of searching for anything we want. We can begin from the places we know best, and search until we get to places we did not even know existed. Or we can begin searching from unknown places until we get to old and familiar places.'

'Which one is better?' The Writer asked, hoping for an easy answer ... just this once.

'How do I know?' her mother said. 'How does anybody know? It is not easy to be wise about these things or make rules about them. It also depends upon what we are looking for. The only thing I can say is that the places that we know well are very few. Those we don't know are many. If you think of how large the earth is, then you can see how small is the part of it that we know well. So if we are looking for something, then it might be better to start from where we know best. Because for one thing, it is not really big. So that if what we are looking for is not there, we would know quite soon enough, and then we will feel free to comb the rest of the big, wide world for it.'

'Yes, Mother. Thank you Mother,' The Writer said.

Hadn't her mother also said a long time ago that it is always better to speak to a young person in proverbs and not just talk to them?

The Writer sighed. She knew the discussions were over.

The Girl Who Can

They say that I was born in Hasodzi; and it is a very big village in the Central Region of our country, Ghana. They also say that when all of Africa is not choking under a drought, Hasodzi lies in a very fertile low land in a district known for its good soil. Maybe that is why any time I don't finish eating my food, Nana says, 'You, Adjoa, you don't know what life is about . . . you don't know what problems there are in this life . . .'

As far as I could see, there was only one problem. And it had nothing to do with what I knew Nana considered as 'problems', or what Maami thinks of as 'the problem'. Maami is my mother. Nana is my mother's mother. And they say I am seven years old. And my problem is that at this seven years of age, there are things I can think in my head, but which, maybe, I do not have the proper language to speak them out with. And that, I think, is a very serious problem. Because it is always difficult to decide whether to keep quiet and not say any of the things that come into my head, or say them and get laughed at. Not that it is easy to get any grown-up to listen to you even when you decide to take the risk and say something serious to them.

Take Nana. First, I have to struggle to catch her attention. Then I tell her something I had taken a long time to figure out. And then you know what always happens? She would at once stop whatever she is doing and, mouth open, stare at me for a very long time. Then bending and turning her head slightly, so that one ear comes down towards me, she'll say in *that* voice: 'Adjoa, you say what?' After I have repeated whatever I had

27

said, she would either, still in that voice, ask me 'never, never, but NEVER to repeat THAT,' or she would immediately burst out laughing. She would laugh and laugh and laugh, until tears run down her cheeks and she would stop whatever she is doing and wipe away the tears with the hanging edges of her cloth. And she would continue laughing until she is completely tired. But then, as soon as another person comes by, just to make sure she doesn't forget whatever (it was) I had said, she would repeat it to her. And then, of course, there would be two old people laughing and screaming with tears running down their faces. Sometimes this show continues until there are three, four or even more of such laughing and screaming tear-faced grown-ups. And all that performance on whatever I'd said? I find something quite confusing in all this. That is, no one ever explains to me, why sometimes I shouldn't repeat some things I say; while at other times, some other things I say would not only be all right, but would be considered so funny, they would be repeated so many times for so many people's enjoyment. You see how neither way of hearing me out can encourage me to express my thoughts too often?

Like all this business to do with my legs. I have always wanted to tell them not to worry. I mean Nana and my mother. That it did not have to be an issue for my two favourite people to fight over. But I didn't want either to be told not to repeat that or it to be considered so funny that anyone would laugh at me until they cried. After all, they were my legs ... When I think back on it now, those two, Nana and my mother, must have been discussing my legs from the day I was born. What I am sure of is that when I came out of the land of sweet, soft silence into the world of noise and comprehension, the first topic I met was my legs.

That discussion was repeated very regularly.

Nana: 'Ah, ah, you know, Kaya, I thank my God that your

very first child is female. But Kaya, I am not sure about her legs. Hm . . . hm . . . hm . . .'

And Nana would shake her head.

Maami: 'Mother, why are you always complaining about Adjoa's legs? If you ask me . . .'

Nana: 'They are too thin. And I am not asking you!'

Nana has many voices. There is a special one she uses to shut everyone up.

'Some people have no legs at all,' my mother would try again with all her small courage.

'But Adjoa has legs,' Nana would insist; 'except that they are too thin. And also too long for a woman. Kaya, listen. Once in a while, but only once in a very long while, somebody decides – nature, a child's spirit mother, an accident happens, and somebody gets born without arms, or legs, or both sets of limbs. And then let me touch wood: it is a sad business. And you know, such things are not for talking about everyday. But if any female child decides to come into this world with legs, then they might as well be legs.'

'What kind of legs?' And always at that point, I knew from her voice that my mother was weeping inside. Nana never heard such inside weeping. Not that it would have stopped Nana even if she had heard it. Which always surprised me. Because, about almost everything else apart from my legs, Nana is such a good grown-up. In any case, what do I know about good grown-ups and bad grown-ups? How could Nana be a good grown-up when she carried on so about my legs? All I want to say is that I really liked Nana except for that.

Nana: 'As I keep saying, if any woman *decides* to come into this world with all of her two legs, then she should select legs that have meat on them: with good calves. Because you are sure such legs would support solid hips. And a woman must have solid hips to be able to have children.'

'Oh, Mother.' That's how my mother would answer. Very, very quietly. And the discussion would end or they would move on to something else.

Sometimes, Nana would pull in something about my father.

How, 'Looking at such a man, we have to be humble and admit that after all, God's children are many . . .'

How, 'After one's only daughter had insisted on marrying a man like that, you still have to thank your God that the biggest problem you got later was having a granddaughter with spindly legs that are too long for a woman, and too thin to be of any use.'

The way she always added that bit about my father under her breath, she probably thought I didn't hear it. But I always heard it. Plus, that is what always shut my mother up for good, so that even if I had not actually heard the words, once my mother looked like even her little courage was finished, I could always guess what Nana had added to the argument.

'Legs that have meat on them with good calves to support solid hips . . . to be able to have children.'

So I wished that one day I would see, for myself, the legs of any woman who had had children. But in our village, that is not easy. The older women wear long wrap-arounds all the time. Perhaps if they let me go bathe in the river in the evening, I could have checked. But I never had the chance. It took a lot of begging: just to get my mother and Nana to let me go splash around in the shallow end of the river with my friends, who were other little girls like me. For proper baths, we used the small bathhouse behind our hut. Therefore, the only naked female legs I have ever really seen are those of other little girls like me. Or older girls in the school. And those of my mother and Nana: two pairs of legs which must surely belong to the approved kind; because Nana gave birth to my mother and my mother gave birth to me. In my eyes, all my friends have got legs that look like legs: but whether the legs have got meat on them to support the kind of hips that . . . that I don't know.

According to the older boys and girls, the distance between our little village and the small town is about five kilometres. I don't know what five kilometres mean. They always complain about how long it is to walk to school and back. But to me, we live in our village, and walking those kilometres didn't matter. School is nice.

School is another thing Nana and my mother discussed often and appeared to have different ideas about. Nana thought it would be a waste of time. I never understood what she meant. My mother seemed to know – and disagreed. She kept telling Nana that she, that is, my mother, felt she was locked into some kind of darkness because she didn't go to school. So that if I, her daughter, could learn to write and read my own name and a little besides – perhaps be able to calculate some things on paper – that would be good. I could always marry later and maybe . . .

Nana would just laugh. 'Ah, maybe with legs like hers, she might as well go to school.'

Running with our classmates on our small sports field and winning first place each time never seemed to me to be anything about which to tell anyone at home. This time it was different. I don't know how the teachers decided to let me run for the junior section of our school in the district games. But they did.

When I went home to tell my mother and Nana, they had not believed it at first. So Nana had taken it upon herself to go and 'ask into it properly'. She came home to tell my mother that it was really true. I was one of my school's runners.

'Is that so?' exclaimed my mother. I know her. Her mouth moved as though she was going to tell Nana, that, after all, there was a secret about me she couldn't be expected to share with anyone. But then Nana herself looked so pleased, out of surprise my mother shut her mouth up. In any case, since the first time they heard the news, I have often caught Nana staring at my legs with a strange look on her face, but still pretending like she was not looking. All this week, she has been washing my school uniform herself. That is a big surprise. And she didn't stop at that, she even went to Mr Mensah's house and borrowed his charcoal pressing iron each time, came back home with it, and ironed and ironed and ironed the uniform, until, if I had been the uniform, I would have said aloud that I had had enough.

Wearing my school uniform this week has been very nice. At the parade the first afternoon, it caught the rays of the sun and shone brighter than everybody else's uniform. I'm sure Nana saw that too, and must have liked it. Yes, she has been coming into town with us every afternoon of this district sports week. Each afternoon, she has pulled one set of fresh old cloth from the big brass bowl to wear. And those old cloths are always so stiffly starched, you can hear the cloth creak when she passes by. But she walks way behind us school children. As though she was on her own way to some place else.

Yes, I have won every race I ran in for my school, and I have won the cup for the best all-round junior athlete. Yes, Nana said that she didn't care if such things are not done. She would do it. You know what she did? She carried the gleaming cup on her back. Like they do with babies, and other very precious things. And this time, not taking the trouble to walk by herself.

When we arrived in our village, she entered our compound to show the cup to my mother before going to give it back to the Headmaster.

Oh. Grown-ups are so strange. Nana is right now carrying me on her knee, and crying softly. Muttering, muttering, muttering. That 'saa', thin legs can also be useful . . . thin legs can also be useful ... That 'even though some legs don't have much meat on them, to carry hips ... they can run. Thin legs can run ... then who knows? ...'

I don't know too much about such things. But that's how I was feeling and thinking all along. That surely, one should be able to do other things with legs as well as have them because they can support hips that make babies. Except that I was afraid of saying that sort of thing aloud. Because someone would have told me never, never but NEVER to repeat such words. Or else, they would have laughed so much at what I'd said, they would have cried.

It's much better this way. To have acted it out to show them, although I could not have planned it.

As for my mother, she has been speechless as usual.

Comparisons

or *Who Said a Bird Cannot Father a Crab?*

Of course, we've heard it said of identical twins. But not only were these two nothing of the kind, they were not even remotely kin. And hadn't we been told of the mysteries of the generation gap? Who were they? One of them was my father. He was my parent. I am his daughter. This other man is my husband. He was not my father's son. So how could they resemble one another so much, at least in those areas that I consider essential to our very being, like our sense of self?

> Here are the numbers that really count . . . ah, but first, it's the news about a friend's house that got flooded in the night's storm, all essential papers and other precious possessions ruined. Of course, it was new. But the developers, including those who walk and work in the name of the state, could not be bothered to use engineers. She needs someone to contact her lawyers, insurance brokers . . . Then there are all those accidents here where half the drivers on the road bought their driving licences and the other half are completely blind, but will not go to have their eyes checked, or cannot afford to, so the corrective glasses are out of the question, no lies or exaggerations . . . We get cancers from the water from ancient leaded pipes that we needs must drink to avoid those dangerous germs and bacteria. The foods that nourish today kill tomorrow . . .

NOW. I pick up my bag. I walk to the car. I am close to tears. The third time this morning. The only reason I'm not screaming is because I don't want the children to see or hear me in that state. No more than I would allow them to stuff their heads with the contents of early morning global news. Right?

FACTS THAT SHOULD NOT CONFUSE, BUT CONFUSE ALL THE SAME. As I said, he was my father. So of course I look like him. Although some people tell me that I am so much more like my mother, 'it's uncanny!' That's another thing. This business of whom a child resembles. It depends on who is doing the seeing, and perhaps what they are quite probably, quite unconsciously, looking for. No? As far as I can remember, all my father's relatives always swore that I resemble my father so much that if I had not been female, I could have been mistaken for him anytime. It's the same tale my mother's people and her friends told. With a little more conviction of course, since with them, there were never any ifs or buts. The question is: if I look like both my parents, and therefore there is no question that my father's blood flows through my veins and all that, then how could he and I have differed so much in all the other ways that mattered? . . . to me anyway?

The wedding had been very expensive, no surprise there. And exhausting: physically, mentally, and psychologically. But that's what weddings are supposed to do to you, no? What the two of us had decided, rather wisely, was that we would go all the way, *dze kaw ato kaw do*, and give ourselves a decent honeymoon, from which we would return to face the debts together. Which is exactly what happened. I don't remember the details of my days the first few years of marriage. I can only talk about these days. Today. Now.

We both work. Me a bank clerk, and he a pharmacist with the Ministry of Health, which means that he works in the dispensary in the central hospital here. We are both paid very badly. He worse than me. That's why any time I hear that a new private clinic has opened in town, I literally run home, or more often to the hospital, to tell him about it. 'I'm biding my time,' he'll say mysteriously. Which in normal language means that he's waiting until the government sends him a letter informing him that he's been transferred from Oguaa. Then he'll hand in his resignation and look for a job with a private clinic in this town. Does it make sense? What I mean is, if something bothers him about his government job, and something obviously does . . . it's the pay. Humiliating. So why doesn't he just quit? I don't know . . . And this isn't the only area where I don't understand my husband.

BACK THEN. I can see him, after his early morning rituals, in his khaki farm clothes. Ah, those khaki shorts and the shirt that he must have worn to the farm over a thirty-year period. When I emerged from babyhood into childhood, those clothes already looked worn and stained. Not nastily, as with splashes of grease and drops of food. But naturally, randomly dyed with the juices and resins of the woods and the farms. All in his day's work. Big patches of stains. Like tie-and-dye. Except that the process had been more organic. Maybe there was more than a pair, perhaps two pairs of them, at least. But when I was a kid, I saw, or thought I saw, only one, the frayed edges of the entire ensemble also seeming a permanent feature.

Banana Republic.
Stylishly elegant on male and female manikins in New York, London and Paris.
The price?
Fat enough.

And I thought, 'How uncanny the resemblance! Did their researchers know him, my father?'

Once upon a time, there was a bright, eager young woman who had been a student volunteer to one of those tropical paradises where both the condemned and the saved live, who, on her return, in a discussion with a friend . . . that friend being an upwardly mobile young man who needed to know where the most exotic and environmentally friendly dyes could be found for his office, a rather well-known design house for outfitting the very chic denizens of the modern workplace, with equally chic, very contemporary, elegant, but affordable rags . . . remembered a place full of indigo trees by a valley where aloes grew wild and lush on the edge of the rainforest. This information, sourced and acted on, had yielded a mighty promotion and a massive salary for one so young, and perhaps the young man on his way to the rainforest for the said indigo had seen my father – or maybe someone else's father – wearing, yes, you've got it, the old, faded, patched and frayed pair of khakis, and being clever and wanting to amaze his company with his gift for innovation and flair, had immediately, and hurriedly, sketched the style, later properly made up. 'Oh, isn't he cool?' . . . his genius received instant recognition, and the rest, as they say, is history.

So there was my father, in his farm fatigues, quite unconscious that he was in the vanguard of high fashion, ready and raring to go and start working at cockcrow.

TODAY. I wake up at 5 a.m., go to the bathroom, then to the children's room to wake them up, which is already a job and a half, prod them towards the bathroom, Abiw branching off to the conveniently separate loo while I drag Nancy all the way to the hand basin where I have to hover around to make sure she actually brushes her teeth. Five years old . . . not that her brother is better at eight . . . And now he is out of the bathroom, so Miss Bladderrock, yes, she is one of those, and what a blessing such are to mothers – touch wood, thank God, inshallah, Ave

37

Maria . . . I leave them in the bathroom, praying silently that they'll get on with their baths, instead of starting an argument so early in the morning about nothing at all. If the tap is running. If it isn't, then I rush to the tanks to fetch Nancy half a bucketful, and invariably collide with Abiw as he is running to turn on the TV. None of my very patient and careful entreaties have been effective. Neither of the two stations here runs programmes for children in the morning. And would you want your children to swallow the early morning load of news about the world's murders, mayhem and general mess with their cocoa?

I dash back to the bathroom to help Nancy with her bath. But before she is through, I have to turn to the kitchen to make sure there is something for their breakfast. Right now, I call out to Abiw that the bathroom is clear, so he can have his bath if the water is running, and if it isn't, could he go for the bucket and take it to the water tank and fetch some water for his own bath, please, Mister? Depending on his mood, Abiw immediately runs to the bathroom for the pail or he pretends he hasn't heard me. It's clearly the latter this morning, so I am screaming the suggestion again, while chasing him to get a move on. At some point I can hear my husband waking up, and rushing to the loo. When he is done, he raps on the bathroom door to ask Abiw to hurry up.

BACK THEN. And my mother? She would have woken up a long time before Father. A very long time. At least, that's how it seemed to me then. In reality, it may have been no more than half an hour, or even its quarter before. She would feed the baby, when there was a baby to be fed, and wash off the night's mess. All this in my father's room, where he had spent the night. Then she would shake us awake, 'us' being my brother Abaka, the firstborn, my older sister, Bosompra, and I, and later, the one who turned out to be our youngest. I remember now, when

38

the last one was still a baby, we older ones had been banished from our father's room, the two girls to sleep in our mother's room, and Abaka to join the other young male relatives in the big hall in the family house at the other end of the village, where they used to raise the funeral bed when any of Father's relatives died.

TODAY. I have put the kettle on to make some coffee for him and tea for myself. I'll take his coffee to the bathroom, or if it's a morning he feels like socializing, he'll join me and the kids in the kitchen so that while they are eating he'll leisurely drink his coffee and demonstrate parental concern by asking the children this and that about school, while I gulp down my tea and try to hurry the children back to their room for them to assemble the contents of their schoolbags – which I didn't manage to check last night because there was no time, or because it occurred to me it was rather late, or I was too tired and sleepy.

Eventually the kids are ready and waiting. So I go back to the kitchen and the small pantry to check what could be available for supper. That done, I aim for the bathroom. He is in there whistling. He comes out, and as he is on his way to the bedroom and me to the bathroom, we collide. He asks me whether I'd put clothes out for him. When I say no, and then turn around to hurry back to the bedroom ahead of him to correct my mistake, I hear him muttering under his breath about how his friends' wives would not do that to their husbands, and I'm close to tears while pretending not to have heard him. So I'm now in the bedroom to put socks, pants, trousers, a singlet and a shirt out for him from a batch of clothes that I had organized for the washman to take away at the weekend, and which that 'other' man had delivered, washed and beautifully ironed. Then it occurs to me, that I might as well lay out some clothes for myself, so I do, and then I rush to the bathroom.

I'm not in the bathroom for even ten minutes when there's

severe rapping on the door, and I hear the gruffest voice – whose owner I couldn't possibly know from anywhere in this world and have definitely not met in any previous existence – asking me when on earth I'll finish having my bath 'because it's getting to half-past seven, and we should have been on our way already.'

BACK THEN. Once we were awake, thanks to Mother's resilience and persistence, we managed to fold our reed mats, and Abaka, our brother, swept the floor. Then we followed my mother. We all walked across the courtyard to my mother's part of the compound where the dirty pots and pans from the previous night's supper were waiting to be washed. I imagine Mother washed the pots before we were born or until we became old enough to do them. I never saw Abaka touch them, even once. It naturally fell to us girls, from I believe when my older sister Bosompra was just about old enough to stand upright, and I was to join her all the time we were at school, and until Bosompra got pregnant and had to leave school to get married, and afterwards, until I left home to go to boarding school.

THIS MORNING. I don't say a word in reply or in my defence, but I notice I am shaking, and close to tears. When I finish and get out of the bathroom I find him sitting in front of the TV watching CNN *Early Morning News* and trying to follow the stock market. On Wall Street, if you please. Sitting in Oguaa, Ghana, watching the New York Stock Exchange and commenting on the volatility or otherwise of NASDAQ. I mean, who has that kind of time in Africa and Ghana, before they go to work? Does that make sense? I mean, what does the wife of the man who's got that kind of time have? Once again, I'm close to tears.

BACK THEN. Mother would first wash the baby, then make the fire and put the pot on to cook the corn porridge. A-h-h-h, that porridge. I remember the way it bubbled while she quickly took her half-bucketful of water to the bamboo bathhouse to wash herself. She came running when she had finished, and on her way back stopped by the fire to check it. Always. She never seemed to miss the routine even once all the time we were growing up. She would then rush indoors to oil her arms and legs and powder the rest of her body, then get into her farm clothes, after which she asked Bosompra or me to go round the corner to Auntie Araba's for bread. When we brought it, she would dish out the porridge. And where was our oldest, our brother Abaka, all that time? Please don't ask me, I don't know. I didn't know even then. Once we left our father's room, Abaka never seemed to be around at all, except when it was time for Mother to dish out the porridge and bread, and later in the evening, when supper was ready to eat. As for household chores, he had one, and one only. Sweeping our father's room. How many chores did each of us girls have? My sister, don't ask me to count them. You too are a girl. You know.

> 'I am the ONLY ONE they send around here,' complained my only child, a daughter. I did not laugh. Not because of her poor siblingless state. I was thinking that Miss Why?-Why?-Why? could have had more than enough reason to sing the same song, even if she had had eleven brothers.

By the way, I am beginning to vaguely remember that if Abaka occasionally wandered by the cooking area, Mother, or some other older woman, would shoo him away, with the threat that 'the boy who insisted on stirring the boiling pot was the one who grew into the beardless man'.

I don't remember Mother or Father eating any of the porridge or anything else in the morning. But I remember that she hurried us on to finish our meal, and hurried us on to have our baths, one after the other, with the water that we had fetched the evening before from the stream, and therefore was very cold. Lord, please forgive me for mentioning your name here, but that water was very cold. I can still feel and hear my teeth chattering down the years until I went to boarding school, where the water that came from the pipes was warmer.

Of course, it was Mother who helped us find our uniforms and our books, and then saw to it that we were really, really out of the house and on our way to school, after we had agreed on where she would hide her keys for the day. From all the Saturdays we didn't go to school, we learnt that after packing us off, she would then go to the market to buy the kenkey and fried fish, tomatoes, onions and fresh peppers, when she didn't already have any of these items at home, and once she was back, wash the grinding stone, grind the vegetables together with salt, which she later packed for Father's lunch and her own, meanwhile having also had to remember to look for the old gallon cooking-oil tin, fill it with water, and add it to the other items already on the wooden tray, and place the tray on her head. Always, always, always, at this stage, with only his machete under his arm, Father would stroll across the courtyard and, with barely suppressed irritation, say to Mother, 'I have been ready to go for these past many hours. No one can call himself a farmer if he sets out for his farm after the sun has appeared to dry off the dew. Esi Achin, what have you being doing ALL MORNING? Why are you women so tardy?!'

Throughout my childhood, those were the first, last, and only words I heard my father speak to my mother in the morning. Every morning, except for two days in the week.

> Dear Father, please forgive me if it wasn't so. I admit that memory is not only selective, but sometimes quite faulty. Although we have each got the memory we've got, and that's the only one we can trust . . .

42

Those were the ordinary mornings, and there were not many such in my mother's week.

If it's morning, my child, then there are debts to pay, group matters to meet about, community work to do, in kind or in cash. And isn't it strange sometimes about night and rest and sleep and waking up to the body's whimpers and wails and screams?

So here are the numbers to count, young or old, there's the sick to tend to and visit, eyes gone dim, ears oozing a burst dam's volume of putrefaction; the sore throat to the clinic; the priest, the priestess, marabout and hospital ... or someone just fell into the well and drowned; some doctored paraffin that caught fire, burnt and killed.

If it's morning, my child, there are the dead for women to dress up, to mourn, to bury, to celebrate.

And when life is good, there's the biggest harvest in living memory to wake up for at dawn, cooking for the annual feast, of the old New Year, Christmas, Idd, the new New Year, marriage to negotiate, a newborn in the neighbourhood.

No, most mornings were not at all ordinary. Looking back, I keep asking myself how Mother managed. It couldn't have been humanly possible to be that busy. Unless one counted Thursdays and Sundays. On Thursday, my parents did not go to the farm, because it was the special day of the god of the land where they had their farms. On Sunday, we all went to church, Mother more regularly than Father. And of course, we had some necessary prodding from Mother.

THIS MORNING. When all the financial news he wants to hear has been read out, fully illustrated and commented upon, he gets up abruptly, and I swear I can feel his legs shaking with irritation inside his trousers. He rushes outside. Soon I can hear the engine of our fifteenth century automobile wheezing and spluttering into life. I can also hear the children running out to the car. I'm all dressed, and my hair is combed out. In spite of everything, I managed to get my hair done over the weekend at the salon, and now I'm wishing I'd had time to give my thick but obedient hair a little more of the attention it deserves. Instead, I pick up my handbag and the carry-all in which I normally haul around all my troubles, commitments, and half of the known universe. That's when the phone rings, and I've decided not to answer it because— and in any case, who's not getting ready to go to work on a Tuesday morning, and doesn't know that other people are?

But he has run back into the bedroom to pick up the receiver and is busy doing his 'ah no' 'ah yes' into it. Only those two syllasomething responses. As if the person at the other end is the other half of this great liaison. But I know better. It's his recently retrenched older brother who is back in the village trying to farm with his settlement, and doing the most ridiculously poor job of it, and right now is phoning to tell him he needs help badly, in fact he just got off the tro-tro, and he is at the station, so could one of us bring him home? And I'm right because my husband is now trying to string some decent sentences together, telling his brother that we are late for work, and the children for school, so could his brother come and wait at the neighbours'. In the meantime, he'll see if he can sneak out later in the morning or early afternoon to come and meet him. I've been waiting for him to finish the telephone discussion. He replaces the receiver. The phone rings again immediately and this time he ignores it too, and that's when he wheels round angrily at me, and says, 'Nora Cobbina,' – only my full maiden name at such times – 'I've been ready and waiting and waiting to leave for my office these past several hours. Remember, I am not a self-employed man, but a civil servant. At least you work with a private organization. So your boss is a human being you can explain things to.'

'Since when?' is what I'm asking in my head.

'Why aren't you ready?' In fact, I am.

'What have you been doing ALL MORNING? And by the way, why are women so tardy?'

> My Sister, please forgive me, but as you and I know too well, even the better times are just an American-style 'good news, bad news' kind of tale: cooking for the annual feast of Christmas, Idd, the New Year; the car for the workshop; airline tickets to buy; a wedding to plan for, or its anniversaries; birthdays to remember, plan for and execute; students off to boarding school . . . My Sister, those pepper pastes take. a hell of a time to cook so they'll keep . . . or it's just the lists, those lists we have to put together for this 'n' that, everything and all, every morning.

Now I'm sitting in the passenger seat watching his face, and noticing how set his jaws are, as he pulls out of the house. It's hard work trying to push the tears back into my head. But I'm determined not to let them fall. It's occurred to me that my tears are too precious to waste. So I open my eyes very wide and stare ahead, aware that my day is ruined. A-h-h-h, here is Mother's face, swimming into focus, sympathetic but also clearly bewildered. Oh, and here is Father's, close behind, a little self-satisfied, almost triumphant?

That's when this cheeky idea occurs to me. That perhaps even the best proverbs cannot apply in all situations, but only to specific places and particular times. So although the ancestors may not agree with me, I think, and want to tell the whole world, that sometimes a crab can father a bird, and at other times, well . . .

Nutty

Later, it had occurred to her that Mistake Number One was trying to translate the names of our foods into English and other European languages, so that foreigners would understand them. End result? You explain the food, and that's not always helpful. Because no one wants to deal with strange ingredients. Especially if they are from Africa. And did she say translate into English? American English, that's what's relevant to this story. Because of the confusion over 'groundnuts' and 'peanuts'. Quite likely, the early American settlers in what came to be known as the South got that nut from their African slaves, and promptly called it peanut. Why? She didn't know . . . hmm . . . maybe it's because it looked like a brown version of their garden pea. 'So many lost facts about so many things,' she mourned, 'or rather, they are ignored, denied and buried.'

The English seem not to have known about it at all. Never did. So naturally, they had no name for it. But then how come their cousins from across the channel seemed to know, and even had a perfectly good name for it? And a lovely name too. A-r-a-c-h-i-d-e.

'Arachide, Aragon. Araras.' She remembered a section of a childish rhyme from a very brief attempt to learn French in secondary school.

'So how come the French have an indigenous name for it and the English don't?' her other voice persisted.

'How on earth would I know?'

'Who first called them groundnuts?'

'Africans, of course . . . Nuts that came from the ground.'

'That's because other nuts grow on trees?'

'Yes, and no . . . No, they are not the only nuts that grow underground. But then our people decided to give the honour of the groundgrown to *nkatse*.'

'Why?'

She did not know. She only knew that her attempt to translate *nkatsenkwan* into English for her American friend a long time ago, when they were both students, had resulted in a fiasco. Because the best equivalent she could come up with was 'peanut butter stew'. It was dumb, she had later admitted to herself. So we can laugh. Really we can . . .

They had shared a rather big apartment with two other students, one from somewhere in Latin America, and the other a white American, like Blanche. The four of them had cohabited rather well. But it was only with Blanche that a genuine friendship had developed. The two of them had decided that they would take turns to cook something special once a month for their Sunday supper. Of course they had to be careful and not let themselves get carried away with complex foods that required fancy ingredients. Their budgets would not allow them to. That's why *akoko-nkatenkwan* was such a good idea. Chicken pieces, a small jar of groundnut paste, onions, a tin of tomato paste, a small piece of ginger, maybe some garlic, salt to taste, and *voilà*!

Blanche had turned quite pale.

'Peanut butter stew?!'

'P-e-a-n-u-t b-u-t-t-e-r s-t-e-w??!!'

Blanche's eyes had narrowed, while her mouth had twisted into a mess of scorn as she hissed: 'P-E-A-N-U-T- B-U-T-T-E-R WHAT?'

You see, Aku-Yaa didn't know it then. That most Americans meet peanut/groundnut for the first time in their lives as a form

47

of butter. Yes, butter is what she'd said. Now it's your turn, world, to say 'What?' Yes, spread on bread, and then topped with jelly . . . jelly? It's another name for jam. She could hear the world asking 'What other word for jam?' So it would only be just to admit that Blanche was right. It was as if Aku-Yaa was offering to make her butter stew, maybe thickened with marmalade, depending on how fast her imagination worked! And clearly, it did.

Aku-Yaa had persisted though, confident in the irresistibility of *nkateewono* – its velvety texture, its bewitching aroma. But you should have seen Blanche's face and her manner as they began to eat that meal. Someone might drink poison knowingly with better cheer. She appeared to be afraid, not just of the sauce in the spoon as she tried to put it into her mouth, but of the spoon itself. Not all their different, equally excellent, breeding could rescue either of them, or the occasion. Of course, once she'd allowed herself to taste it properly, she lapped up what had been in her bowl, and sure, even took a second helping. Couldn't seem to get enough of it. But nothing in all of Aku-Yaa's life before or since had shamed her so much. She must have recovered, the young do, but the scars must be some of the largest and most raised keloids in the world. That was about fifteen years ago. Aku-Yaa didn't know how, or why, they had kept in touch. But they had. It must be in the way some relationships refuse to die, no matter what. They had kept in touch through their postgraduate phases, while they looked for work, Aku-Yaa ending up teaching at the polytechnic, getting married very late, and now she is nearly 50, with a daughter and a son, who are really quite young at 15 and 13; Blanche, on the other hand, landing what she had described to Aku-Yaa as a sweet job, working for an oil company, and insisting on staying single, 'No kids please, not if I'll have to get pregnant first, and I shall never adopt. Can you imagine the hassle?'

As usual, when Aku-Yaa knew for certain that she was going to be in North America for about a month, she had sent Blanche all the relevant details. Once she was clear about her pro-gramme, the different places she would be staying at while attending meetings or visiting friends and relatives. In line with a by-now-established tradition, they had agreed that her friend would come to take her out for a meal. Over the years, Blanche would sometimes join Aku-Yaa at her hotel for a simple supper on her way home from work. At other times, she would come for her African friend and take her to her latest trendy eatery. Angus beef and fluffy mashed potatoes à la mountain butter, Mexican fried beans deluxe; *nouveau* won-ton; they've done some.

However, that evening was going to be different. Blanche had come to pick up Aku-Yaa from the hotel to take her home. On the way, they had chattered as usual, about this and that; how much more frequently the friends seemed to be travelling than before, how Blanche's meeting in Marrakesh was, and what a pity it hadn't been organized somewhere else lower down the Sahara, so that they could have met on her African soil for a change.

Aku-Yaa had been taking advantage of the free tickets and usually free accommodation that came with her international travel to make a little money on the side, selling cloths and clothes to contacts she had now firmly established in different cities. But somehow, she had never tried to share that side of her life with Blanche.

In response to a question about her children, Aku-Yaa had answered eagerly enough. The kids were really growing. The boy was already a year into secondary school, and the girl was getting ready to follow from the beginning of the next academic year. She was just starting on a little self-pitying about how she wished she had had her children earlier than in her late thirties

49

when Blanche reminded her crisply that as they were talking, a fifty-four year old woman somewhere was expecting triplets. Then they both burst out laughing with relief and wonder at our changing world.

The relief had been from other tensions, other sources. You know how these things happen without warning, between old friends? Especially old friends? Especially when they are from different parts of the world? Different cultures? Silently judging one another? And the judgment getting in the way of affection? And then if you are an African, you learning to accept all the other definitely uncomfortable, and quite often humiliating and senseless complications, and undercurrents?

So the relief didn't last. At all. Because one second they were laughing, the other second Blanche was telling her friend that in her honour she had tried her hand at a new exotic recipe, and the result was outstanding. A stone dropped into the pit of Aku-Yaa's belly. Just like that. Where had the stone come from? Aku-Yaa had no idea. An 'exotic dish'? She'd been travelling widely around the world, and long enough to know by now that these days the exotic means:

strange, weird, dumb:

both those who dress strangely, as well as the apparel they don, clothes that are described as costumes though worn outside the theatre, and for everyday living; accents that are so thick their owners might as well have spoken in their native tongues and saved themselves and 'us' the trouble; entire cultures to which the term modern can never apply . . . people who refuse to deal with the Internet.

Then they were pulling into Blanche's carport. Aku-Yaa had always thought her friend's home was beautiful, told her so again, and meant it. Shining clean, contemporary décor. Her two cats and one big dog seemed to be exquisitely groomed, while everything else looked elegantly cheerful and welcoming. All quite festive really.

'I thought I would treat us to a leisurely four-course meal,' Blanche announced enthusiastically, after asking Aku-Yaa to make herself comfortable.

A four-course meal. Hmm. Aku-Yaa tried to relax, and not be silly. She was not going to allow herself to feel bad that where she came from, sometimes even a one-course meal was a problem for many to achieve. 'Aku', she crooned to her inner self, 'just relax, and enjoy yourself.'

Sure enough, Blanche served a really delicious salad with shrimps and avocado pear, and then brought in the main course with a flourish. Before Aku-Yaa could crane her neck to look, it had completely announced itself in very certain terms. The aroma was unmistakable: it was *nkatsekwan-na-akokonam*. Chicken done in peanut butter or groundnut paste. It had to be that combination. Because, in spite of its own highly distinctive and strong aroma, no soup or stew prepared with peanut butter (groundnut paste) had the same smell as any other that was concocted with different ingredients. Peanut butter with beef is one thing, with chicken another, and with lamb yet a third, and on and on and on . . .

Aku-Yaa woke up from her dream to Blanche's invitation that she served herself. Apart from the pot of stew, there was a dish with steaming white rice, and some cold cut and grated vegetables for accompaniments. She murmured in pleasurable anticipation. However, as she began to spoon some of the sauce on to the rice she had taken, she noticed that the preparation was slightly different from the type she was familiar with. The chicken had been boned, and the meat cut into morsels. She also discovered that there were whole and half peanuts scattered through the sauce. In spite of that slight unfamiliarity, Aku loved it. 'Same taste as our version,' she thought. 'Except for a slight difference . . . and what is that?'

Hmm . . .

Hmm . . .

Hmm . . . hmm . . . hmm . . .

Then it clicked. This was American supermarket chicken cooked in bottled American peanut paste, smooth and creamy. Wonderful, but somehow different from the end-product at home, made from a combination of similar but slightly more natural ingredients. In fact, apart from those whole and half nuts, this was exactly the version she'd cooked for Blanche in the apartment they had shared when they were students. Same, same same.

She had to ask. 'Blanche, what's the name of this . . . this . . . wonderful, exotic dish?'

'You like it? . . . The name . . . I'm not sure I'll get it right if I try to pronounce it . . .'

Her friend's reaction was quick, easy, almost nonchalant.

'And where did you get the recipe from?'

'Actually from another friend,' she said.

'Where does your friend come from?' Aku-Yaa had to know.

'Frankly, I've never bothered to find out.' Blanche was sounding slightly uncomfortable. 'You know how it is. These days, you can't just go asking where people come from, seeing most of us can come from anywhere.'

'Ah . . . huh,' Aku-Yaa murmured guiltily, but not satisfied. And Blanche caught her mood.

'By the way, why do you want to know?' She was clearly uneasy now. Because it might have occurred to her that normally, if we encounter some new food we like, what we do is ask for the recipe. not where the recipe has come from.

Aku-Yaa had to bring it out. 'Because I've made it for you before.' She hoped she had not shouted, or sounded angry.

'What? When? And where?' Blanche was completely taken aback. Aku-Yaa reminded her, taking her time, and the trouble to keep her voice innocent. Only the bare facts. Meanwhile, Blanche's face was mirroring only one of the different regions of the mind she was passing through. She looked genuinely surprised.

'You don't say!' And, now knowing how to interpret that, Aku-Yaa just said, 'Yes.'

She could hear strains of a popular highlife band, which she had once heard introduced on a radio station as 'world music'. The presenter had mentioned the band's name, but not where it came from. As though crediting the music with Africa would somehow take something away from it. What she had felt then was not shame exactly. Must have been confusion. And here she was, with a delicious meal ruined for her, and thinking that in this global village where African music is only part of 'world music', maybe African food becomes edible only when it is part of an exotic universal cuisine.

She told herself she shouldn't stress herself out. It was only food. So she giggled daintily, and went through the rest of the evening with a tight smile on her face. Glued to her seat, Blanche too had a tight smile on her face. But she couldn't allow herself to stay glued to her seat. She was the host. So she bustled around. After the main course, she presented Aku-Yaa with cheese and crackers, as well as a fantastic ice-cream ensemble she said was called tropical Arctic bomb, all the while repeating the mantra: 'We are forgetting calories and cholesterol tonight.'

They must have continued eating, and finally washed everything down with some excellent liqueur. 'It could have been such a nice evening,' Aku-Yaa was thinking ruefully as they got ready for Blanche to return her to the hotel.

Blanche swore to herself that 'Next time, it will be fried chicken, corn on the cob, and mashed potatoes,' as she remembered, with a meanness that surprised herself, what in those faraway student days, Aku-Yaa (she was Rosemary then!) had claimed was her favourite American meal.

'Gross.' She didn't know she had whispered that aloud until her friend turned to her with a questioning look. 'I was thinking aloud,' she explained unnecessarily. By then both of them knew they had to end that particular evening fast. It had begun to go from disaster to disaster, and clearly, and once again, not all their different but equally excellent breeding could rescue either of them, or the occasion.

That was last month. As she went up and down, getting ready to return to North America before the end of the year for one reason or another, Aku-Yaa was wondering whether she would still have the energy to look up her friend. Meanwhile, she could not have known that for once, Blanche too was dreading her friend's next trip to North America, whenever that would be.

Such sad residents of the global village . . .

She-Who-Would-Be-King

(with an apology to Rudyard Kipling)

An encounter that took place in the kitchen of a university guest house. Half a century earlier, in 1977.

He-of-25-years-old:

'So what did you say you will be when you grow up?'

She-of-10-years-old:

'The President.'

'The what?'

'The President.'

'The President?'

'Yes.'

'Of what?'

'This country.'

'W-H-A-T-?-!-!'

'Why not?'

'You are mad.'

'No.'

'Well, you can't be.'

'Yes, I can.'

'You are mad.'

'I am not.'

'Anyway, you can never be the President of this country.'

'Why not?'

'Listen, I don't think the men of this country will ever let a woman be their President.'

'No? We shall see.'

And now, the year is 2026. The month, May. The day, the 25th. The old woman is 86 years old. Her daughter, the lawyer (whose story this should have been), turned 59 six months ago. Her granddaughter (whose story it turns out to be) would be 36 at year's end.

The 'Old Queen', as the family calls her behind her back, is lying in the adjustable chair in the corner. The members of her family think that she is old beyond joy and sorrow. So they have arrived at an unspoken agreement. That the only way she can jubilate with them over this most welcome but still unbelievable piece of news is for others to fuss over her. So they keep fiddling around with the contraption, rearranging now her pillows, now the headrest . . . Then before she can open her mouth to say she is fine, someone comes to raise – or did he lower? – the foot-rest.

But the plain truth is that she really is quite comfortable. In fact, if anybody had ever told her that a day would come when she would feel this much at peace with herself and the world, she would have laughed in her face. Her life has been very difficult, and full of surprises that were not always pleasant. She could never plan her life. So time had often taken her into some awkward places. But then this is not supposed to be her story . . .

Her daugher is Adjoa Moji, Professor and Dean of the Law Faculty. Her students call her Prof. AdjMoj, affectionately, behind her back. She is in the house but not in the family room. The Old Queen cannot see her. But she can feel her.

There are, at least, four generations of the family in the room, as well as representatives of several different branches of it. Actually, it is not a room as such. It is really the square open space linking the four sides of the house, roofed with glass, and a huge skylight created in the process. So that as you approach from the garage you are pleasantly surprised to find yourself entering a classical African clan courtyard, which is also a lounge in the European style.

The house itself, built with a loan from the university, is rather small. However, its design is so original that it has become a subject of intense discussions among the Professor's friends and colleagues, as well as members of the general public. Suddenly, everybody is an expert on architecture. Of course, those who don't like the Professor, or envy her and her family, say that the thing looks and feels like a hothouse.

The television set is in the centre of the room facing west. Its screen is as wide as the screen for a small lecture theatre. This is 2026, so of course it's high-definition. But since this is 2026, the Anane household's screen is neither the biggest nor the highest defined around. In this neighbourhood near the university campus, people are not the poorest in the country, but they are also not the richest. In fact, in the real 'cash-dey' sections of this city, some homes have got teevees with screens that are almost as wide as those that used to be in the old cinema houses in the city centre. So that as soon as the sun goes down, the skies in such areas are lit by the glare from the television sets. Yet this is only a state capital. They say that in the capital city of the Confederation of African States, there are many more such neighbourhoods. Those who have been there claim that in fact, even if the city council was to stop providing street lights at night, the total glow from people watching their teevees would be enough to light the streets.

Of course, the first name that everybody had originally thought of for the union was the United States of Africa. But then everybody had also agreed that that would not do. People would want to abbreviate it. And when they did, it would be 'USA', and of course, everybody knew Uncle Sam would not like that. So the formal abbreviation in English is CAS. But one trait which survived with the Africans who survived the unspeakable twentieth century is their cynicism, and the capacity to laugh at themselves. So they have already begun to call the union The CASE.

The capital city has had to take all of the last twenty-five years to recover from the previous thirty years of civil war.

It isn't Africa's capital alone that went through a rough time. The entire continent had gone through hell in the last forty years of the twentieth century, and the first ten years of this century. She had been in hell of one kind or another for exactly five hundred years. But those fifty were something special. Man-made but accidental, man-made and deliberate, home-grown, imported, natural ... Name it. If it was a calamity, Africa suffered it.

At the height of the AIDS epidemic, the priests from the different religions had had to set up camp in the cemeteries from 8 o'clock in the morning, and did not leave until late at night. To cheer themselves up, everybody had joked that burials had become the hottest 9 to 5 job in town with no pay for overtime.

Then there was The Drought. At its worst, those who were paranoid had said that white folks were fiddling with the planet.

'They are fixing Africa to face the sun permanently . . .'

'. . . to deprive us of rains.'

'They are trying to fry us.'

'. . . part of the Great Plot to wipe us off the surface of the earth. So they will be free to take our continent completely. Instead of just holding on to it by devious and vicious means, as they'd been doing the last five centuries . . .'

The real tragedy was that in those days you could find plenty of support for such fears and very little to discount them with. However, others had talked then of the 30-year drought cycle. Most of them knew nothing for certain. They were only doing some wishful thinking. But a few had been geographers, weather people and other such sundry experts. Anyway, to our general relief, those who belonged to the latter, more optimistic group seemed to have been proven right.

Almost on the dot of 1 January, 2010, the rains started. From the Cape to Cairo, it rained, and rained and rained. The Nile, the Niger, the Congo, the Zambezi and all our rivers swelled and overflowed their banks. And so had the great lakes: Chad, the Volta, Victoria and Kariba had filled up again. Even the Sahara and the Kalahari began to green up. Of course, that wasn't going to last. The deserts were not going to become rain forests. But the illusion that they might stay green, like they did at the beginning of time, was not bad for our spirits. Hope was long coming. Now it was here, and we held on to it, every which way we could.

The Old Queen knows that at this very minute, AdjMoj is in her bedroom, dancing before her dressing mirror. That is, if the high jumps, wide armthrows and feet-kicking she does when she is happy can be called that. How well she knows this child of hers!

Her mother is right. AdjMoj is dancing. What else can she do? On a day and in an hour like this? She can hear her grandmother, a long time ago in the village, muttering to herself whenever something nice happened, or she heard a piece of good news: 'Tarkwa ewu ntsem muo!' Oh yes, it must be unfortunate to die early in Tarkwa. Or anywhere else for that matter. She has remembered the saying because she has lived long enough to see this day, and not just her. Even Mamaa has lived long enough to see this day.

The main news has come on. And sure enough, Afi-Yaa has been elected the first President of the newly formed Confederation of African States.

An encounter that took place in another part of town, the evening of this same day of 25th May, 2026.

He-of-74-years-old:

'Did you watch the news?'

His son, in his 40s:

'Who didn't?'

'Hmmm . . .'

'She is only thirty-six! . . . And they say her grandmother is eighty-six, tight like a wire, and lucid like the edge of a razor blade.'

'But is a razor blade really lucid?'

'Eh . . . hm . . . well, it's sharp.'

'So her grandmother is 86, and sharp like a razor.'

'Anyway, that's it. We are going to have her for the next one hundred years!'

'Why do you think that?'

'This is Africa, isn't it? No one resigns here. Certainly not heads of governments or any outfits for that matter. And they never allow themselves to get voted out of power. Not if they can help it. No, they are either thrown out in coups, or they sit on people's heads until they rot with old age. And those who wait in the wings as deputies or the opposition are no better. Sometimes they even manage to be worse.'

'That was quite a speech. But wake up. These are the 2020s. Not the 1970s or the 80s or even the 90s. In any case, it was I who lived through all that. Not you. So, shut up. And she is a woman.'

'What difference does that make?'

'Should be a lot. Those were power-hungry old men . . .'

'. . . and power-hungry young men . . .'

'Okay. Well, she is a young woman, and she doesn't seem to be hungry for anything. Least of all power.'

'No? We shall see.'

'. . . hm . . . that's what her mother said to me a long time ago.'

'Her mother?'

'Yes. I know her.'

'You know her mother? That professor?'

'Yes. Or rather, I knew her then.'

'How? . . . Where? . . . H-o-w?'

'It's a long story . . . And why are you so surprised?'

'Well . . . well . . .'

'Well what? You know something? Some things clearly do not change. She is a university professor who has built a cottage that is supposed to be the most interesting house in town. And I am only a manufacturer, a businessman . . .'

'With lots of money and the biggest house in town!'

'No, we didn't leave our prejudices and other pettiness in the twentieth century. What a pity! . . .'

'Please, Father, I didn't mean it that way . . . Stop being so sensitive about your wealth and tell me about you and this girl's mother.'

'Okay. You just said "No? We shall see." That's exactly what the mother said to me one day, when I told her that the men of this land would never let a woman be President.'

'She wanted to be the President of this country?'

'Yes. Or at least, that's what she told me when she was ten years old, and this was a country.'

'Now her daughter is the President of Africa!'

'The First President of Africa.'

'Good Lord!'

'Don't swear . . . The Ancients have said that it's the same thing if a horse doesn't go to the battle front, but its tail does.'

'Good Lord!'

'Didn't I ask you not to swear? Wanting to be corrected at your age like a little boy! And remember, that girl is your President . . . In fact, as my workers at the site would insist: "contri chief be President, all Africa chief no be President: e be

61

King. So as for this woman, e be She-King." ... My son, you better look for a more decent way of referring to her even in private.'

'Good L-o-r-d!'

Heavy Moments

*In a salute to Millicent Melody Danquah, Ayele Komey
and Joanna Araba Maanan Dickson, the three women who
first dared to join the Ghana Air Force. The last one was
disqualified from flying because of severely defective
eyesight. But the first two definitely became pilots.*

Akuba opened the door to the toilet near the cockpit. She had
almost waited too long. Because she was now having to do a
little *tinawale* jig. Left foot down, right foot up. So that she
would not wet herself. There was no time at all for her to stop
and wonder at the phenomenon. How could this happen to her
of all people? Her Mampa had always warned her against what
she described as Akuba's habit of senselessly and uselessly
hoarding her urine. 'One of these days, you are going to burst
your bladder.'

Akuba nearly choked on that. 'Oh Mampa,' she thought
fondly. She was also remembering that it was the same Mampa
she had once overheard mutter to herself that we meet our in-
laws only when we are in our farming rags. Or something to
that effect. And in any case, is this the time to remember all
these things? But the mind is a funny thing. So she went on
remembering as she struggled out of the trousers of her uniform.
She had worn a brand new pair. Which in retrospect could not
have been the wisest thing to do. The zipper was proving
difficult . . . please God, don't let it break. Please God, don't . . .
then the trousers were unzipped, she was sitting on the toilet,
and peeing what appeared to be all the clear fluids from her

63

body. This was obviously a morning of surprises. Now where had she heard the one about the old man who, in an argument as to whether women should wear trousers, had calmly declared, puffing on his pipe, that it should not really be a problem for anybody but women themselves? 'If they want to imitate men, fine. They'll find out whether they should wear trousers when they want to urinate!'

Enjoying the release of the tension at the bottom of her belly, she flushed the toilet, washed her hands, shut the door of the toilet and returned to the cockpit. She sat down, smiled at her co-pilot and took the controls. The captain nearly made some comment about women. But he bit his tongue. Biting his tongue had almost become a habit in the past couple of years that he had had those two among his recruits at the Air Force Academy. Suddenly, everything had changed completely. Whereas before, you could say anything you liked about women and be sure of a sympathetic ear and a good laugh, these days, you had to watch everything: your step, your mouth and over your shoulder.

Earlier, they had thought it wouldn't matter. But it had come to matter. Terribly. At first, an alarm had sounded through the academy when first the rumours, then later the hard facts, had come out. Two of the very best candidates that year were women.

'Women?'

'Women.'

'But . . . but . . . but . . .'

'What do they want here?'

'What do they want here?'

'What do they want here?'

Everybody had asked the same questions. From retired Group Captains who had only heard of it at the mess which was still their home from home, to those recruits who were as new to the academy as the young women themselves. It had never occurred to the questioners that Akuba Baidoo and Sarah Larbi wanted from the Academy what they too had gone there for. That if being a flying soldier was something to be enjoyed and lived by, then other people – including women – could want it too. They had even tried to ignore the two young women recruits and carry on as if they were not around at all. Or at best as if the two too were men. So during the first term, even those who would ordinarily not have been given to telling lewd jokes, went around looking for some to tell. Especially when 'Cadet Baidoo' and 'Cadet Larbi' were around. And no one had liked it that 'the girls' did not laugh.

At the end of the semester, Akuba and Yaa Sarah had complained to the Director of the Academy. He himself had been one of the worst offenders. So although he had been careful not to tease 'the girls' to their faces, he had listened them out, and then tried to pretend that he had not the slightest idea of what they were talking about. It didn't work. So he had promised he would do something about it. He subsequently called his lieutenants, spoke to them, and asked them to speak to their men. There followed a period when, except demanded by the most formal of circumstances, virtually no one spoke to them at the academy. When they compared notes during that time and later, each of them made an admission. That if she had been alone, she would have given up and left. But luckily, they were two. So sticking it out had been a little easier.

And now here is Akuba handling the manual controls of an air force plane, as though she had been born flying. Good God, a woman. Wonders surely would never cease.

Actually, Akuba had been born flying. Except that in her environment, no one had known that except herself. Her maternal grandparents' village lay in the path of the planes that flew over coastal West Africa: from southern and central Africa on

65

their way to North Africa and beyond to Europe, as well as those that flew from those northern places to the south. One of the most enduring memories from her childhood was of her and a group of children from the neighbourhood watching those planes. In fact, she was certain that the earliest sound she had caught as a foetus in her mother's womb was the drone of a plane passing over the distant skies ... Now she knew that those planes flew at over thirty thousand feet high. But clearly, that had not stopped her and her friends from rushing out if it was during the day, and screaming their usual chorus:

Aeroplane e!	'Dear plane, dear plane,
ekor aa to paano	(on your return journey)
brem oo!	buy some bread and
	bring to me, oo!'

It was quite possible that for some of the other children, it had just been another game they played. Maybe for others, it had been an expression of a desire to travel. Because one didn't have to send a plane that high up and so far away just for bread? Especially since Auntie Araba baked the best bread in the world right there in the village? Besides, there were several more bakers in Dominase. And one had not even gone as far as Mankessim and Oguaa yet, where for sure, they used to say, there were so many bakers you sometimes wondered who bought whose bread? ... But she also remembered that the grown-ups always said that whatever came from overseas was very special. So maybe, that included b-r-e-a-d?

However, as far as she was concerned, aeroplanes had always meant something different.

She had wanted to fly them.

The desire had been in her for so long, she could not tell how early she was when she became aware of it. All she knew was that one night – it must have been deep, deep in the night – she had woken up suddenly to what was unmistakably the sound of a passing plane. And then she knew she wished she was up there flying it. When the sound of the plane died, she started to cry. When her big mother Mam'Panyin asked her what the matter was, she couldn't speak. She just sat there wailing. In exasperation, Mampa had called her a witch of a child, wailing in the middle of the night. Did she know it was a taboo? A bad omen? Because all the bad spirits will come and join in, and then someone in the house or neighbourhood was bound to die for sure? When she still couldn't stop crying, Mampa had given her a surprising knock on the head. So Akuba had bitten her tongue and wet herself. Mampa had felt so bad, she had taken Akuba in her arms and rocked her, and started to cry herself. Because you see, even as a young child, Akuba never wet herself. It was a terrible night. Finally, both of them had slept again only in the early hours of the morning.

But she had never forgotten that night, and now here she was actually flying a plane and so excited she nearly peed on herself.

She was lucky. At mid-morning in September, the sky was brilliantly blue. And although they were about fifteen thousand feet up, they could see into everywhere and forever. Ahead, the sea that was the Gulf of Guinea reflected the brilliance of the sky. To the right and left, the forest was giving way to low savannah. She knew she would have to get ready to land the plane very soon. She was almost sorry. Not almost. She wished the plane was one of those futuristic self-fuelling machines that could go forever on ordinary air. Or at least, one of those then being planned for American presidents which its designers claimed would be able to refuel in midair, and then fly non-stop for eight days or something monstrous like that.

Supposing she failed? She panicked so much she nearly made

a mistake. She bit her lips. Her hands were shaking, and she soon began to sweat. She told herself not to be silly. If she failed, she would take the exam again. Then she reminded herself that given their environment, getting a place in the academy at all was hard enough. She was not sure they let people stay there forever, taking their own good time to graduate. And had she forgotten she was a woman? One of the first two ever in the history of the Academy? How much would her failure be regarded as personal and nothing to do with her gender? All in all, she had better pass this test.

Until she came to understand it all later, she had always assumed that Mam'Panyin was her grandmother. But it had turned out she was not. She was her mother's older sister: her grandmother's first child. And in fact, that was why everyone called her Big Mother. There had been about seven or eight more children between Mam'Panyin and her mother. Her mother had been the last but one of her grandmother's children. The last, a boy, had been so big, her poor grandmother had died during his birth. Or soon after.

As for her mother who was then only two years old, they had packed her off to the coastal town of Sekunde: to a distant educated relative who had promised to look after her like her own. But in the end, the educated relative had just used the little orphan, as soon as she could run and fetch, as a slave for her household. So the child that was to be Akuba's mother was never put into school for even a day. But the relative's children had gone on to become doctors, lawyers and such . . .

Then one day, the little orphan had bloomed into a young beautiful woman, and the next, a young railway worker in the neighbourhood had made her pregnant. When the educated relative discovered the pregnancy, she had packed Akuba's mother back to the village. When Akuba's natural father journeyed to the village to get things sorted out properly, her mother's people had refused to give him even a place to sit down. Hearing him out was out of the question. How could they marry their princess to someone who lived in a city where human beings could be so cruel? No way ... They say Akuba's natural father later drank himself to death.

After Akuba was born, her mother, who had been hurt and hurt and hurt by all these goings-on, decided to take her child back with her into town. And things had gone well with mother and child until Akuba's mother got married. And then the man said he didn't want Akuba around. Whereupon she was sent back to the village, where she went to school until she was about twelve years old. Then marriage or no-marriage, Akuba's mother decided that Akuba should go back to live with her and take the Common Entrance Examinations. So that was how she got into secondary school. But her stepfather hadn't really changed. Except to indicate that if he had to have this step-daughter around, then he would sleep with her. And if she would not let him, which Akuba would not, then he would beat her to death. That was the last time Akuba saw her mother's house in Sekunde. She never set foot there again. From boarding school, Akuba went straight to Mam'Panyin in the village, deciding somewhere along the way that if she had got parents in this world, it must be Man'Panyin for a father and Mam'Panyin for a mother. But as a kid, she had never been able to say 'Mam'Panyin'. She had arbitrarily abbreviated it to 'Mampa'. And so that's how the whole village came to call Mam'Panyin 'Mampa'.

It was all very well for Mampa to complain about Akuba behaving as though she belonged in the air. But the fact was that Akuba did feel airborne. Always. Or something like that, anyway. She had never felt rooted. She had never felt like she belonged on the ground. There had been this business of getting passed around all through her childhood, between the village and the town. And, of course, when she was in the village, everyone accused her of having 'funny town ways'. And when she was in town, everyone had laughed at her for being 'bush', 'a villager'! Not having a 'proper mother' or a 'proper father' like everyone else was only part of the story.

Poor Akuba. She could not have known, could she, that in any group of people, one clear quarter or more were in some similar situation?! . . .

No, the skies had to be better.

Of course, there was a bit of a crisis when Akuba went to tell Mampa that she had been accepted at the Air Force Academy. Mampa thought it was all too much.

'I say,' Mampa said, 'if I told people that you are going to learn to drive a lorry, a taxi or a bus, they would think it is strange, but brave achievement enough for a woman. But how do you expect me to go and tell anybody that you are actually going to drive an aeroplane through the skies and be believed? And if they won't believe me, what's the use in trying to tell them? Eh, my lady?!'

They had planned everything. That her test flight should be on that day. It was risky. You took such chances only with the best of the cadets, since you had to be able to guarantee success on about 90% probability. But then Baidoo was one such cadet. They were very sure of her. And Cadet Larbi and such among the male cadets who could remotely be described as Baidoo's friends had said how much Akuba loved her aunt, and was always talking about her. So the administration had decided that since this was going to be a rare enough occasion, testing a female cadet pilot (!), they might as well go all the way and do something extra special. They would let this old lady know about Akuba's test flight: the date, the time, everything. Yes, they would take the responsibility to alert her, and leave it to her to decide whether to come to the air force base or not.

The voice from the control tower came over the radio clearly, helping, guiding. She began to gently nose down . . .

Then she was actually taxiing on the airstrip. She brought the plane to a stop. She realized that there was quite a crowd waiting for her. In no time at all, the captain and everyone who had been on board were already on the tarmac, looking up at her as she came down. And they started clapping, and then the small crowd at the edge of the airstrip was also clapping. All her colleagues were there. Each one of them. Those who had already had their tests, and the rest who had been scheduled to come after her. They were all there. Waiting. Then someone broke into that mad English song: 'For she is a jolly good fellow . . .' Everyone took the song up. And she wanted to tell them, 'Silly, can't you see I am not a "fellow" at all? Jolly or not?' How had all these men managed to change so much within such a short time? After all they had put her and Yaa through? How could they show their joy for her so clearly? And by the way, where was Cadet (Yaa) Sarah Larbi . . . where was Yaa Sarah? Akuba wanted to burst into tears, with both joy and . . . yes, disappointment. God, where was Yaa Sarah? Someone was opening a bottle of champagne. Then she could see Sarah coming out of the crowd. Ow-w-w, what a relief! And with her an older woman. And ow . . . it's Mampa, Mampa, Mampa . . .

Some Global News

A short four-voice report

For Pamela (Waterman), a New Yorker of
Caribbean parentage, who genuinely feels dizzy
at the thought of wearing print. No kidding.

It is reported that stress levels are exceedingly high in
anyone born a twin in southern Ghana, who finds them-
selves in Europe or North America on a Friday, after
September First.
Why is that?
In a moment, please . . .

Yaa-yaa Mensah has wished she could open up to Kate about
what is bothering her. But then, how can she, when she has not
completely sorted out the issue for herself yet? So as she prepares
to meet Kate this afternoon, she is a little worried. That to her
friend's most harmless questions, she would respond with out-
bursts. Her irritation would show. Which she knows is unfair:
taking her frustrations out on the one person who probably
understands her more than anyone else. Including her own
children. And these days, Yaa-yaa is learning to be careful with
those two. Even now that they are in their twenties, they seem
to think that the divorce was somehow their fault, or she
certainly blames them for it, and therefore, doesn't love them
anymore . . .

Hmm, how can life manage to be so complicated?

And now here is something else so much more complex, she simply does not know how to handle it. And that is saying a lot about her present state of mind. Because one fact she had known about herself since she was a kid was that she seemed to have been born with an inability to see any aspect of life as a complication. There was nothing she had ever wanted to say to anybody which she had not said. And she does not remember anything she had wanted to do which she had not done. If she hadn't said whatever or done it, then she had not really wanted to. Not badly enough. But now, here she is, struggling to deal with the idea of the global village, so she can discuss it with her friend: where the idea came from, and how people like her are expected to handle it. What she would like to know is, whose village is it, anyway?

Kate Hagan is truly puzzled by Yaa-yaa. What has got into her friend? she wonders. Since she returned from her last trip to America – or was it to Canada? – Yaa-yaa has been so irritable, it's become practically impossible to talk to her. Of course, Kate suspects that plain old fatigue could be having a lot to do with it. 'And none of us is getting any younger,' she reminds herself wrily. 'At our age, we should be slowing down . . . at least a little.' But their lives were not at all easy. 'Busybusybusybusybusy . . . Busybusybusybusybusy!' is how they have come to greet one another these last couple of years.

But even within the unbelievable busy-ness of their lives, and the lives of just about everyone in their circle of relatives, friends, schoolmates and colleagues, there is a solid opinion that Yaa-yaa has given herself a particularly punishing schedule. Kate knows this because they have been close for a very long time. She also knows that people gossip about her friend all the time. How mad she was to have left her job teaching at the university college . . . Of course, it didn't pay well enough to take care of her financial commitments. These days, whose job in this country does? – But it was one of the more secure ones, and a little more comfortable too. Subsidized housing, long and short vacations . . . not bad. Yet what does the crazy woman do but up one day, resign from her job, collect her meagre gratuity, move out of the university bungalow, rent a place in town and just when everybody was wondering what she was about, we hear she had gone and formed her own NGO and now look at how busy she is!

'Her own NGO?'

'Whatever is that?'

'What is on that NGO's agenda?'

'What I would like to know is what is on Yaa-yaa's agenda?'

'But why are you all talking as if you didn't know Yaa-yaa? Wasn't she always a little funny? . . .'

Depending on who was doing the talking, any or all of this was said with affectionate censure, critical exasperation, or envy. Meanwhile, the subject of all this gossip either knew nothing of it or pretended she did not know. 'I am in my late forties and if at this stage in my life, I don't have the courage to venture out and do something which I've wanted to do all my adult life, when can I? From now on, I can only die or get old!'

Kate had thought her friend could try and be less ridiculous. But then, she had also had to remind herself that the decision to resign from the university and start something on her own could not have been made lightly. It had cost her friend what everyone had thought of as an excellent marriage of twenty-something years. 'But that, my friend, is another l-o-n-g story,' they would scream together, earlier sadly, and lately hilariously, sometimes, even giving one another 'fives'.

Yaa-yaa had called her outfit VENTURE 16. The idea, according to her, was simple. She would create a small office where young sixteen-year-old girls could come for advice about life

74

and how to live it. 'Nobody is doing that sort of thing for them these days,' she would add by way of an explanation. In the end, everybody had agreed that it was a brilliant idea, while also wondering how she was going to finance it. That had proved very tough indeed. At least on three occasions, she had considered giving up. 'And then do what?' she had asked herself, her children had asked her, her mother had asked her and Kate had asked her. At the time, she had had no answer for anybody. Going back to the university was out of the question. So she had pressed on. That was in the first couple of years of VEN-TURE's life. Then her numerous and tireless applications to government agencies and foreign funding outfits began to attract attention.

Six years later, VENTURE 16 has grown so much that it is squeezing the very life out of Yaa-yaa. The biggest complication, also the least foreseen, is the travelling. These days, it seems as if there is no governmental committee to look into anything, but they need the input of that 'new organization': Non-formal Education. Dealing with National Service Absconders. Negative Environmental Impact on Mid-teens, just . . . name it. Of course, a whole army of people had joined VENTURE 16 or Yaa-yaa has brought them in, as more hands were needed. These include a board of directors, as well as what she refers to as her troops: a revolving number of sixteen-year-olds whom the office itself employs on all manner of temporary/part-time bases. Just as the end of each school year brought in a fresh pool, the beginning of the new school year sent out the previous batch. Now there are also about a dozen or so more permanent older office staff. Finally these days, VENTURE 16 gets a regular stream of mothers and an occasional father, who are so impressed with it they volunteer their time to do whatever they can to help: on the premises, in their homes, or in the community. We have not talked about the international angle yet. Which is where the hardest of the travelling comes in. Because out there too, it seems as though there is no workshop, conference, caucus on young women, or the youth in general, to which this African NGO would not be invited. As much as possible, Yaa-yaa lets other VENTURE 16 personnel and associates do some of the work and represent the organization. So it is the combination of what she thinks must only be done by her, or where she absolutely has to go, which is killing her now.

Who lives in it?

'But girl, if it is a global village, then everybody lives in it, an-eh-h-h?'

'Ah-h-h-, but someone must be making the laws that rule the village?'

Of course . . . of course.

She had tried to figure it out while waiting at Heathrow to connect with her flight home. Then she had realized that she was too tired to think straight. The last session of the conference had gone on too long. So by the time they came to pick her up to go to the college where the audience of students were waiting to hear her, she knew that for once, it was too much.

Maybe, it's all getting to be too much?

There was that voice again. But she clenched her teeth, shut that stupid and lazy inner voice up, had a quick shower, changed, and was ready.

The organizers of the evening knew that with 'so many events competing for the attention of the campus, expectations for filling a lecture hall for any Third World speaker, not to mention an African, should be modest.' And they had chosen wisely. As Yaa-yaa walked to the front of the hall, she noticed that the room was almost filled to capacity. That had acted like a booster shot, and she had given a very good speech and a brilliant performance.

It is reported that for some reason, from ancient times, people of the tropics, that is, people who live in hot climates, have always preferred hot food: hot as in both with heat and spiced, while those who live in colder regions liked cold food: cold as in without heat and cold as in bland, unspiced ... It should make sense then, (shouldn't it?) that people from warm climates should prefer 'hot' clothes as in bright and printed, while those in colder climates would feel more comfortable in solids and darks as in 'cool' ... Or even 'cold' garments?

But that should be no news!
Are you kidding?

Yaa-yaa had thought that the question and answer period that had followed her presentation was going extremely well. Some members of the audience were clearly interested in the contents of her lecture. There was even this young man who had triumphantly announced that he had spent some time in West Africa, and had emerged as some kind of an expert, and who had tried to use up the entire questions and discussion period. That had been a little irritating. Happily, the others didn't quite let him. So what had turned out to be the last question had taken her by surprise.

'Ms Mensah, you have just told us that the young people of your native land are caught up in problems like high rate high school dropout, teenage pregnancies and drugs. And these are problems our very highly industrialized country is also facing. So if Third World countries and First World countries are facing the same problems, then can we agree with those who think the world is now a global village?'

Third World. First World. Global Village?

She found the implications of these concepts rather disturbing, and the ease with which young people in these countries bandied them around even more so. There was evidence that they had internalized what the concepts implied. That is, if they were the first world, then naturally, they were superior: and if we were the third world, then we were inferior.

And who, by the way, are Second World, and how did they qualify?

A by-product of all this was an arrogance that was truly amazing. Young people who were much much younger than your own children, stopping you in your tracks and surprising you with the most incredibly personal questions and expecting you to give them answers. And if you did or didn't give the expected answers, then you had them acting like, 'How dare you?' Meanwhile, she had noticed that over the last few years, the people at home too, including the youth, were using the same terminologies and internalizing the converse implications: to the extent that she had got into her own little personal panic. Because the result was a kind of galloping post-colonial lack of confidence – or loss in self confidence – does it even matter which? – that was distressing and fast becoming alarming . . .

Post-colonial? . . . Aha, here comes another terrible one to watch out for. Watch out, girl, watch out. Whom do you talk to? Where does one go for help? The rules are getting laid out all right. Take clothes.

If, some years ago, anyone had told Yaa-yaa that clothes are political, she would have laughed out aloud. Now she knows better. Everything is political and everything about clothes is political: the fabric they are made out of; the dyes on the fabrics; the cut; who does the cutting, and on and on and on ... Otherwise, why should she find herself in such a bind? And she is in a bind. When she realized some time ago that she would be doing a whole lot of travelling, and may even have to spend about a total of half of every year attending conferences, workshops and other meetings in all sorts of climatic zones, she made a decision. She would put together a wardrobe of clothes which she could wear both at home and abroad. Although she had come to this decision on her own, it was not a new idea. Other women from the tropics who had found their lives divided between their home countries and colder places had come to the same realization ...

Women from the 'tropics'?
   Did you mean underdeveloped-stroke-third world countries?

And why are all those 'colder places' also mostly to the north of everybody else and mostly more developed?

... it was the most convenient way to handle the problem. You just made your clothes. You wore them to work, to meetings and such places. Then when you had to travel abroad, you packed a few, took along a sweater, a light jacket, a heavy coat, gloves. When it became necessary, you supplemented your clothes with whatever was appropriate for the temperature. It should have worked. But it hasn't.
   As part of what the two of them describe as Yaa-yaa's re-entry programme, they meet to eat *fufu* with groundnut soup ...

You mean peanut soup? or rather, peanut broth? The colonizers made sure us people called some ordinary vegetables by different names. One wonders why ... Maybe to help us maintain a little more of our primitiveness, however well we spoke their language? Or, and to make certain that we never really became that familiar with it?

... at Kate's place, the first free weekend they can have together.

It is their ritual, their secret wicked meal, all the more enjoyed because a real good pot is about a million calories a mouthful. So now here they are, sitting comfortably on the carpet on each side of the coffee table, with the huge 'unladylike-bowl', according to Kate's mother, between them, and the two bottles of beer Kate would normally chill for the occasion.

'Why do you say that your neat arrangement with clothes doesn't work?'

'Because of the rigid notions people in those places have about clothes.'

'Is that so? ... and why is that?'

'Well ... I have come to learn, in a hard and humiliating way ...'

'That?'

'That cotton dresses, made from vividly coloured prints, with wide-necked blouses, are for wearing in late spring and the summer only.'

'When it's warm and bright outside, no doubt?'

'Yes, when it's really warm and bright outside.'

'Ow, if that is what summer is, then in our country it's summer all the time and such clothes are appropriate.'

'Of course, but then do they know that, and if they know, do they care?'

'So, what do they wear the rest of the year?'

'Plain colours. They call them solids. Light greys and browns in early spring and autumn, and black, dark browns, dark reds and other very solid darks in the winter.'

'Ugh, you definitely can't wear such things here just for everyday living . . .'

'I know.'

'Still, nobody can tell you at a conference that you should not wear your clothes?'

'Not in so many words. But they do all the same.'

'How?'

'Well, look at this. You are attending a conference in Chicago, Toronto or Liverpool – wherever – in January. There is a lot of snow on the ground and it is very cold. So you are wearing some heavy boots, and under your *kaba* you have on a sweater, and over all that a very heavy coat. Meanwhile, your hands are encased in gloves and you finished the whole business off with a muffler, or a scarf, to cover your neck and shoulders. Fully confident that you are well and properly attired for that time and place, you enter the meeting room which, as is often the case, is in a windowless, built-to-conserve-energy skyscraper. Once in, like all the other participants, you first take off the gloves, then your overcoat (which you must always remember Americans call jacket) and hang it. Now the rest of your clothes are revealed. Immediately, two or three voices chime out:

"Oh, how pretty!" . . . But hear: "How exotic"!

"How nice and summery!" But hear: "This is terribly inappropriate."

"You sure make me feel this winter has stayed way too long." But hear: "You really shouldn't be wearing these clothes. They are loud and silly." '

'Really?'

'Really.'

81

'But it sounds so unfair!'

'It is . . .'

'Oh, Yaa-yaa.'

'. . . And it doesn't help any when someone thinks she should be honest with you, and says something like: "Hi, you are looking gorgeous but you must be freezing." '

'That's because it's so cold outside?'

'Yes, but then it would only be cold outside. Inside where we would be, the place would so well-heated that everybody would be complaining about how hot it is.'

'So what can you do?'

'I don't know.'

'Are you saying that they are telling us we live in a global village, but only some of the people are expected to make the necessary adjustments so we can all continue to live in it?'

'That's how things seem to be working out right now.'

'How terrible!'

Kate is unable to keep the sense of tragedy out of her voice. No wonder her friend has been so unhappy. What she is wondering though – in fact has always wondered – but knows she can never give voice to, is how come Yaa-yaa and people like her are going on these trips to places like America and England and Germany all the time . . .

> And now they have added Japan, Hong Kong, Malaysia and South Korea to the list.

. . . if they get so very unhappy when they get there? I mean, look at the simple matter of what to wear? The last bit escaped her lips.

Yaa-yaa is cutting into Kate's thoughts.

'Ei, ei stop there. What to wear has never been simple. Not there. Not here. Not anywhere.'

'What do you mean?'

'I am talking about the other half of my story.'

'You mean there is another half to all of this?'

'Oh yes.'

'What do you mean?'

'And how many times are you going to ask me that today?'

'Yaa-yaa, I'm sorry . . . for sounding so stupid.' Kate says this very meekly, in her little-girl 'please-Mummy' voice.

'Kate, I'm sorry,' Yaa-yaa too offers.

'What do you mean?'

'What I mean is, you see, Kate, for me, the whole situation has become such a problem, it alone may stop me from travelling overseas.'

'Well, well, well. Trust my sister to react so drastically to something so small.' Kate whispers this too. Loudly, she says, 'If that's how you feel, fine. Come join us who have never even seen the inside of a plane before . . .'

'Who is now exaggerating?' And they both laugh at the joke.

'But really, Yaa-yaa,' she continues after a pause, 'do you have to stop travelling because of clothes?'

'Let me explain,' Yaa-yaa offers again. 'Recently, I tried to get a whole lot of clothes made here which I thought should suit the taste of the people over there. But then, that has only added to my troubles.'

'What do you mean?'

'I mean that moving between all these places is next to impossible because of all the rigid notions people here too have about clothes.'

'You believe that?'

'I don't believe it. I know it . . .' She is actually shouting.

And that is one thing you simply don't do when you are eating groundnut soup. You begin to choke.

83

Yaa-yaa is coughing and Kate is hitting her on the back. 'Take a big gulp of beer,' Kate orders Yaa-yaa. Yaa-yaa obeys. The coughing stops.

'You see, all the clothes I got made were from dark prints,' she starts again, her eyes glistening with unshed tears. And Kate wonders whether they are from the coughing or from the frustration of it all ... 'Yes, they are from dark prints: black, navy blue, deep red, purple, metallic brown.'

'But Yaa-yaa, those are funeral colours!' Kate exclaims confidently with the full weight of tradition behind her. Then there she is, in the next instant, covering her wide open mouth, in a horrified recognition of just what she too has just said.

> It is further reported that some eminent team of researchers have discovered that darker-skinned people are attracted to bright clothes, and ...

Of course, light-skinned people prefer darks?
'Yes.'

'C'mon, that shouldn't have required the attention of any "eminent team of researchers"?!'

'No ... Maybe not. But it does not seem to be obvious to the dictators of international fashion ...'

'You mean the fashion dictators of the Euro-American world who dictate for the rest of the world, anyway?'

'Right ... Right! R-i-g-h-t! ...' Yaa-yaa is exclaiming, in open triumph.

'I am not going to ask you what you mean by that.' It's confession time for Kate.

'Even if you don't, I'll tell you anyway,' replies Yaa-yaa as if it's a life and death threat. Now it is Kate who is trying not to panic.

'Really?'

'Really.'

'Oh, Yaa-yaa! . . . anyway, so exactly what do you mean?'

'I knew you were going to ask me what I meant again.' Yaa-yaa is not even pretending not to be dramatic as she continues: 'My Sister, in a place where people ask you who has died when you wear a pair of black trousers, putting together a wardrobe of dark clothes is asking for trouble. From humans . . . and the fates too.

> Because from infancy, your mother would have drummed into you that as a demi-god, for whom Fridays are celebration days, you should be in completely spotless white clothes or at the very least, in something white, every Friday.'

'And why can't you in Europe and North America?'

'Because in those places, it is considered a crime to wear white after September First.'

'Why?'

'Because summer is officially over from that date. Autumn has begun and why would you want to be so perverse as to insist on still wearing anything bright? As someone said, if you don't mind appearing crazy, at least, think of your friends.'

Kate cannot look at her friend in the eye. Between them, the *fufu* and soup has gone cold a long while ago. When Yaa-yaa's hand accidentally touches the food, she withdraws it quickly. Kate looks at her quizzically. It is on the tip of Yaa-yaa's tongue to explain that the food is *frozen cold*. She checks herself

85

though, as she remembers that here in the tropics, nothing ever gets *frozen cold*. Things just go cool. Then as decay sets in, they heat up again.

'Yes, girl,' says her inner voice, 'in this global village, nothing is the same for everyone: and that includes language.

'Especially language,' the voice corrects itself.

About the Wedding Feast

With a little warning for all those who may be
allergic to the genre: that this is 'kitchen literature'
with a vengeance. AAA

It had begun with the announcement itself. That those two were
going to get married. My granddaughter just came in from her
workplace one early evening and told us. No asking. It was all
telling. That was when something hit me. Yes, from that early.
That there was something not right already. In the old days,
when things were done properly, a girl did not just announce
that sort of thing in that sort of way. But later, when I pointed
that out to the child's mother, my daughter Mary, she said that
things have changed.

Hei, and how they have changed! ... And of course, being
my daughter Mary, hard as a palm kernel outside and coconut-
soft inside, she later came and without apologizing for speaking
like that to me, asked me how the young lady should have
informed us about what she and her young man intended ...

And then there was the matter of the time. How can a serious
discussion like marriage intentions start at the end of the day?
In the old days, if a young woman wanted to bring up such a
matter, she would begin by just hinting to one of her mothers
on her mother's side, who would hint to her mother, who would
then have hinted to me her grandmother, and then I and her
mother would have discreetly mentioned it to any other mothers
and grandmothers whom we considered close enough to be
brought into the discussion and the negotiations that would

follow. Then, very early the next morning (at dawn really) we would have had a meeting, in my room certainly, sitting down properly, of course . . . But here I go again, forgetting that things have changed!

In this case, the young lady came to just tell us. And that was how everything got handled. In the modern, educated way, and not at all properly.

Maybe I should not have let myself grieve: since for a start, we were in a foreign land. The young man my granddaughter was going to marry is from one part of Africa that is quite far from our country. My daughter Mary had sent me a ticket to go and visit her and her husband and children. Indeed, let me tell the truth: when it comes to such gestures, Mary is good. So I had gone. As everybody knows, this was the second or third time. In fact, I was preparing to return home here when the announcement came from my grandchild. That was a blessing. Because, the way things have changed, I could sense that they were going to go ahead and finalize everything, when no one at home had the slightest knowlege about the proposed marriage. And then, what was I going to tell everybody when I came back? You would all have laughed at me, no? That I too had gone and lost my head abroad: the way all these educated people seem to do when they travel overseas.

So I said to Mary, my daughter: 'Mary, it is true that things have changed, but have they really changed that much?'

'Maybe not, Mother . . . you only worry too much,' was what she said. Now tell me, what kind of a response was that?

Anyway, that was when I came back here and informed you all about it. I had been quite surprised and very relieved that you had such understanding. Was it you or Abanowa who had suggested that since the child was in a foreign land anyway, and the young man she was marrying does not come from anywhere around here, everybody should accept that there was no question of anybody getting the chance to go and check his background to make sure everything about him and his family was satisfactory, and so if I found him acceptable, that should be fine with you all? At the time, I had not commented on it, but oh, I was so grateful for that.

As I had informed you all at the family meeting, I knew Mary was going to be sending me a ticket to go back there for the wedding. But she had sent it much earlier ... Mary doesn't know how to do a lot of things. In that she is not alone. It's the education. It takes away some very important part of understanding from them. But then, I must also say for Mary that those things she knows how to do, she does them very well.

So, that was how I came to be present at the big meeting between Mary and the boy's mother about what should be prepared for the wedding feast ... To tell the truth, I had not really felt too happy at the idea of a joint discussion. It was not right. What self-respecting family in the old days would ask for help from their prospective in-laws? Whether it was in the way of just ideas or for something more substantial like the actual preparation of the food for the wedding feast? But when I so much as opened my mouth, Mary said that these days, that is not only all right, but even expected. She added that in fact, she might hurt feelings if she didn't ask for the help. Mmm, things have really changed, haven't they?

Since there was not going to be any grandmother from the boy's side at the meeting, Mary and I agreed that even though I would sit in on the discussions I would keep a respectable silence. Which was what I did. However, every now and then, my daughter whispered questions to me to which I gave discreet answers. It had not seemed as if there was much disagreement about anything. They had discussed everything in a friendly way: the wedding cake itself; other cakes; biscuits and buns;

how to do the groundnuts and the other things for the guests to munch and crunch . . .

Groundnuts? Oh yes, they are everywhere! Except that in most places, they call them peanuts!

They had sat and talked for a long time, maybe for as much as half the day, when they came to the foods that called for real cooking. That was when things began to take time to decide. I had been thinking, and even told them, that if they did not stop for a little rest and get something to eat, something nasty was going to happen. But Mary said, and it was plain the boy's mother agreed with her, that it was better to finish everything at a sitting. I was going to open my mouth and tell them that since the beginning of creation, no family had finished planning what should go into a wedding feast at one sitting. But then I remembered that things have changed, and warned my lips.

Then it happened and I was not at all surprised. I had heard Mary mention *jolof* and other dishes from our country. Then maybe, for just the shortest bit of time, I had got lost in my own thoughts and had not paid attention to the discussions. Because I had not noticed that something had come up which was really cutting their tempers short. All I saw was suddenly, Mary and the boy's mother standing up at the same time and each of them shouting:

'That's no food and you are not serving it at my daughter's wedding.'

'That's no food and you are not serving it at my son's wedding.'

'Spinach stewed with a mixture of meat and fish?' shouted one with a sneer that was big enough to wither a virgin forest.

'Spinach stewed with only onions and without meat or fish?'

shouted the other, the contempt in her voice heavy enough to crush a giant.

'What do you mean?' shouted one.

'What do you mean?' countered the other.

'I said that's no food, and you are not going to serve it at my child's wedding!' they both screamed at the same time.

'You cannot tell me that,' one wailed.

'You cannot tell me that,' the other whined after her.

'Our guests will not eat that,' one spat out.

'Our guests will laugh at us if you serve that,' said the other.

'They will tell everyone in our community.'

'They will write home to everyone in our country about it.'

'It is awful, a mess.'

'Yours is unclean.'

'Yours is completely tasteless.'

'But you ate it when you came to our house?!' said one, perplexed.

'But you ate it when you came to our house?' said the other, equally perplexed.

'No, I didn't, I didn't touch it,' they both confessed.

'Eh?!'

'I went and threw it into the rubbish bin in the kitchen.'

'W-h-a-t?'

They made as if they were going to clutch at each other's throats.

'Mother, Mother, what is this?'

None of us who were already in the room had seen or felt my granddaughter and the young man come in. But they had.

'What is this?' they repeated. The mothers stopped dead. Shame on their faces, each stared at the girl and the boy in the hallway. For what had seemed to be a very long time, there was complete silence. Then the boy and the girl looked at one another, burst out laughing, didn't stay to say anything else to anybody and then went out of the room, still laughing.

What did the mothers do? What could they do? Each of them just sat down and stayed sat. And quiet. After some time, I called my daughter Mary's name.

'What is it?' she asked, glaring at me.

'Listen,' I said, my voice low. 'I think you people had better stop now and continue with the planning of the feast tomorrow.'

'What is there to plan? . . . Anyway, I am finished with all that,' Mary said. And with that she went out of the room.

And that's how everything ended with the food affair. Oh yes, there was a wedding. And it was not only the ceremony itself that went well. Everything else was wonderful. We cooked our *palaver sauce* of spinach with *egusi*, meat and fish. The boy's people cooked their very plain spinach, without meat or fish . . . And did the guests eat? Don't even ask. They ate and ate and ate and ate. Since then, I have not heard that anyone from the boy's side complained about the food we cooked. And I am not hearing anyone from our side complain about the food our in-laws cooked . . .

You see oh . . . what still puzzles me is how people can tell others how much things have changed, when they do not prepare their own minds to handle such changes, eh . . . And as my mother used to say:

'What is food anyway? Once it goes down the throat . . .'

Lice

Life has its problems. Without further ruining one's already bad nerves listening to The World News first thing in the morning. And when you are

> just a woman,
> an ordinary wife with a normal marriage,
> ignored, double-timed –
> a harassed mother,
> a low-paid teacher in a rotten,
> third world educational system,
> What should you want The World News for anyway?
> It's like eavesdropping on gossip about humankind. In this last quarter of the 20th century, you are bound to hear something nasty. If not about your own backyard, then about some other people or some things you are stupid enough to care greatly about . . .

Sissie knew she should know better. Which she did. But then, doing better is another task altogether.

She had been prepared quite well for the life everyone had suspected she was going to have to lead. Her mother had advised her to remember counting her blessings. Actually, that was not her mother. That had been the kindly missionary nuns who ran her old secondary boarding school.

> They scurried among them
> like frightened white mice

in a tropical forest,
forever surprise in their eyes –
yet
still managing to
fuss,
like all mothers

And from her mother:
'My Child, don't complain
so much. Always remember
that it doesn't matter how
bad your situation is, someone
nearby is wishing they were you.'

Sissie's eyes flew open against her will. So she quickly shut them again. Tightly. Sissie knew she was awake. She also knew 'Baby' was lying by her . . . Really, she should stop herself and everybody else calling the poor child 'Baby'. After all, she was a grand old lady of five years. Plus she had got a name . . . names.

The countryside of Euro-Africa and Afro-Europe are indeed cluttered with . . .

Ah no, she shouldn't start on that sort of track this morning. Instead, she should start counting her blessings.

One: She had got a husband: married to traditionally, legally, fully . . . She could remember the wedding. She could also remember the events leading to the ceremony . . . Her Big Mother murmuring, 'Now our daughter has become a proper lady. Ah-h-h, our daughter has become a proper lady!' while she tried, Big Mother would, to adjust the veil here, push a curl from the wig there . . . All in an attempt to beautify things a little more, no doubt. But then Big Mother had ended up just upsetting the semi-professional wedding merchants hired for the occasion.

The ceremony itself that night . . .

Just as without looking, Sissie knew her second child had crawled into the bed some time in the night, she also knew without looking that her husband was not occupying his side of the bed. In fact, he had not been home at all. And that made the third night he had not been. She knew he had been sneaking into the house when he was certain that she had gone to work. He would always need a change of clothes before going to work, at least.

She wondered what stories he was telling at his workplace to explain his regular lateness . . .

The mind too is a countryside cluttered with rubbish. Why couldn't she mind her own business? Concentrate on her own troubles? Keep on counting her blessings?

Two. She had the children. Kofi was seven, and 'Baby' Afua Anamua was five. One boy, one girl.

> 'Wo *mmpɛ yei*
> *Na*
> *Wopɛ deɛn?*'

'If you aren't grateful for this, then what the hell do you want?'

There were always two queues at the clinic. One was pregnant:

— Women with just missed periods, seeking confirmation.
— Women at mid-term, looking for general good health for the remaining half of the trip, for insurance against post-partum disasters . . .
— Women at full term. Only a few weeks or a few days due. All eyes shining, nostrils flared with certain exulta-tion: the very toes in the sandals oozing with fulfilment.

The other queue, which was always twice as long or longer, was infertile or completely barren. Everyone in it was looking for a child. An addition to, or replacement for the one or two born some time ago, and which had lived or died. Or because they had never had any. Ever.

— Young working girls whose tentative experiments with unplanned sex had not ended in the half-dreaded, half-desired pregnancies with which they had hoped to trap the relevant young men into marriage.
— Women who were actively looking for pregnancy. Their marriages depended on it. Their femininity. Their humanity. They were always very fashionable: well-dressed, delicately perfumed, their figures well-kept, and since their men refused to go for check-ups with them, who knows, perhaps the doctor himself or some other male accidentally met leading to a quick accidental you-know-what? and leading to a baby . . .
— Women who had lost all hope. But who still kept going back to the clinic. As much to keep appointments with the doctor as with one another. For wasn't it only here that they could still be regarded as human beings? So that they too could chat, exchange confidences and trade gossip?

Sissie's eyes were still tightly shut. Briefly, she asked herself where counting one's blessings ended and dwelling on other people's woes began?

Three . . . three . . . three . . .

She could only remember her son, the inside of his school shorts soaked with blood. She wondered, very briefly, whether Blessing Number One would have bothered to come home if he knew their son had hurt himself falling off a tree in school . . .

96

The Nursing Sister on duty at the hospital had made jokes in an attempt to keep her calm, perhaps.

'Madam, we have been very lucky. Just think of it, what could we have done, if it was the precious weapon that had been ruined? Such a handsome young man too. Think of it: what would our daughters have done? Ha, ha ha!'

Sissie had not felt at all like laughing.

'Madam,' the Nursing Sister had continued, 'please hold his hand.'

Sissie remembered taking hold of Kofi's hand. She remembered asking what they were going to do.

'Ah, Madam,' Nursing Sister had crooned, 'We are so lucky. So-o-o lucky. We have a little bit of antiseptic left, and we will clean the wound with it. But unfortunately, that's all. It is not serious enough to put him under general anaesthesia. And we don't have anything for a local either . . . We'll give him *pethidine*. That will relax him. But please, could you hold his hand while we stitch the wound up?'

Sissie's eyes were still tightly shut. In the darkness, she remembered clearly that the nurse's assurances had put her feelings under general anaesthesia. She had felt absolutely nothing for the next half hour. Her son had been screaming and screaming. And then after she had covered his mouth with her cupped hand, he just whimpered like a dying animal as the needle went in and out of his flesh. While the black silk thread looked unimpressively familiar. Nothing about it to say it wasn't the regular cotton used for plaiting hair and bought from the city market . . .

Blessing Number Three: she had a job.

This time, Sissie's body experienced a major spasm. Yes, the ring and the 'Mrs' title had produced one definite result. She did not have to be nervous entering the headmaster's office any longer. He had obviously taken the hint. Plus there were all those younger and juicier unprotected females that made a third of the student population . . .

Of course, she was beginning to live with the knowledge that as long as she taught in that school, the headmaster was never going to recommend her for promotion . . . Dear God, and her salary stayed the same, while inflation daily shrunk its value. The whole lot would now not pay for one dress . . . But wasn't there something quite universal about that these days?

At her old school, the advice had been even in the form of a song they used to sing. Something to the effect that

'Count your blessings
Name them one by one . . .'

Yes, at least, she had a job. She could see the secondary school where she taught. With more than twice the number of students it should have had in the dormitories; empty science laboratories, other empty places that should have been equipped; the pipes that were perennially dry from the drought, or leaking the little water away with old age and rust . . . Even chalk was often a problem. Sure, nothing much was coming from the Ministry. But she also knew that the little that came was equally shared between the headmaster and the bursar. From food for the boarders to exercise books and chalk. Well, they too had other mouths to feed and relatives to impress.

Ugh. Sissie shuddered again.

Blessing Number Four. It was a Saturday. No school.

But she still had to take Kofi to the hospital to have his wound seen to. And how was she to do that? The hospital was on the other side of town. The car was definitely with Blessing Number One who had no doubt parked it outside the door of whoever's bed he had been sharing these past nights.

The car was half-broken down. Like everybody else's. But

when it moved, it was a car. Half the money that had gone into buying it had been hers. You wouldn't guess it, would you? From the way she had to beg for rides in it? Her mother had called her a fool when she had told her about their plans two years earlier. Sissie had felt hurt at first, and then secretly consoled herself that her mother was only an uneducated villager who could not be expected to understand the intricacies of a modern marriage . . .

On a Saturday morning, no taxi driver was going to drive to distant places from the centre of the city. No, not on his hard-won petrol, his threadbare tyres, his half-working gears . . .

So how was she going to get Kofi to the hospital?

And when did she do the weekly shopping before the shops closed down for the weekend? And it wasn't even a question of dashing in and out of the shops, picking this and that . . . The city market was still good: Thank God. But the shops! She would have to stand forever in the queues which no one paid any attention to, since she fell into no easily identifiable grouping.

She did not look obviously pregnant.

She did not carry the card of an ex-serviceman of the World Wars.

She was not a senior army or police officer.

She was not an important businessman or businesswoman.

She did not have any political connections.

She was not the manager's relative,

his wife, or

his girl-friend. And

She was not . . .

Oh Mother-Superior, why didn't you ever add that counting blessings can be quite a hard job too?

She should have gone to the bathroom a long time ago. Her bladder was full and hurting. But that would have meant some eye-opening. And she was not ready to face the world this morning. So her eyes remained tightly shut as she moved to lie flat on her stomach. Her mind told her the dawn was breaking since the shiny, moving black things in her head were gradually turning to grey, spangled moving things. A happy bird was twittering somewhere nearby. A happy bird.

'Mammy . . . Mammy . . . Mammy!'

'Yes "Baby", what is it?'

'Wake up.'

'Why?'

'Mammy, just wake up.'

'Oh please, I am so tired.'

'Mammy, wake up.'

'"Baby", I am very tired. And it is not morning yet.'

'Yes, it is. Look!'

'Please "Baby", leave me to sleep a little.'

'Mammy, wake up and sing me a song.'

Sissie's eyes remained tightly shut. Maybe the bird outside was singing because her child wanted her to? Except that she knew this morning she could not sing no matter how much her daughter pleaded.

'Baby' crawled from her side and threw her body across Sissie's back.

'Mammy . . . Mammy . . . Mammy, my head is itching.'

Without opening her eyes, Sissie reached out her left hand and touched her daughter's head.

'Here, here, here,' cried the little girl. 'All over, Mammy.'

Sissie opened her eyes.

She reached out, moved 'Baby' off her back, turned over and sat up. It was still not light enough to see the itching head.

She realized she had to run and go to the bathroom if she was not going to pour the contents of her bladder on the bed. She sighed. She put her feet on the floor.

'I am coming back,' she told the little girl and ran out of the room.

On her way back from the bathroom, she went to peep in at Kofi. He was still sleeping. She touched his forehead. It was not hot. She left the room and shut the door softly behind her. Back in the bedroom, Sissie switched on the single overhead bulb. 'Baby' was still scratching her head. So Sissie asked her to sit on the floor while she had a look. She parted the child's hair at random. A huge louse was crouching on her scalp. Sissie groaned as she picked it and crushed it. She parted another part of the hair. She saw two lice. True enough, the little girl's hair was full of lice.

Sissie began to shiver. And then she felt funny in her stomach and on her chest. 'I am coming back,' she told the little girl again and ran out to the bathroom. She held on to the wash basin. But she was not sick. It was just nausea. Apart from the fact that her skin felt damp, she was all right. She also felt her eyes beginning to smart with unshed tears. She quickly washed her face.

What was she to do? No she wasn't sure what to do about what. As she walked back to the bedroom the second time, she met 'Baby' on her way to the toilet.

Sissie sat on the edge of the bed. 'No one should feel as I am feeling right now, so early in the morning,' she told herself aloud. That was when she realized her own head was itching. She began to scratch it. But the more she scratched, the worse it got. Then 'Baby' returned from the bathroom, sat on the floor again like she remembered her mother had asked her to. One hand was in her hair, a finger of the other hand in her mouth, her eyes raised with some expectation at her mother. Sissie let herself fall back on the bed, closed her eyes again, but this time with her scalp itching very badly. From the floor, 'Baby' began to wail again, 'Mammy, Mammy!' while Sissie's own mind whined: 'What am I going to do? What am I going to do?' She had not realized she had switched on the little transistor radio. But surely enough, the news was on:

... President Reagan had won a landslide victory for a second term as President of the United States of America, ... There had been a monstrous explosion at some nation's petroleum depot in (She had missed the name of the city and the country) ... hundreds of people were feared dead ... hundreds of surrounding homes were destroyed ... thousands evacuated ... World experts do not see the end of the drought in sight. In fact, Africa was in for a worse time next year. All that can be predicted was more of:

the appalling pictures of emaciated children
the victims of war
the columns of refugees trailing across
dusty landscapes into
urban squalor ...

Then she wasn't sure anymore whether all of that was coming that minute out of the radio. Or was it her mind doing funny tricks with other bits of the news heard at other times? In any case, the room had begun to spin a little.

Sissie took hold of herself. Suddenly, she knew what she had to do. There was a little paraffin left in the gallon can.

Where had she heard that paraffin was the best remedy for getting rid of lice?

She went to the corner of the garage where they kept things like paraffin ... It wasn't much of a garage. Just a small open shed to protect the car from the rain and the sun. They normally backed out straight from it into the street. But it was better than nothing ... She picked the gallon can and returned to the bedroom. She looked for, and found, the wide-toothed wooden comb, and carefully combed 'Baby's' hair. Then she combed her own hair.

When she removed the lid from the gallon can, the fumes of petrol jumped at her. She had picked the wrong petroleum product. She paused for just a fraction of a second . . . After all, if paraffin can get rid of lice, petrol can do that and much more? . . .

Petrol should get rid of some of life's problems.
Petrol gets rid of some of life's problems. All of life's problems.

She soaked her little girl's head first. Thoroughly. Then she soaked up her own. She was by now in so much haste, the stuff was spilling on herself, over the bed, on the floor . . .

Where were matches?

She was feeling too tired to walk all the way back to the kitchen. But there was no need. On the dressing table was one of Blessing Number One's discarded match boxes. She jumped and picked it up.

'Baby' had sat through all that petrol dousing without a murmur. Now, she said: 'Mammy, it smells.'

'Yes, "Baby", only for now. Soon the smell will go away.'

How should she go about it? Ah, she knew. She should light 'Baby's' head first. Then her own. She struck the match. Loud coughing came from beyond the door. Of course, it was Kofi who had coughed. There was also a sound of him turning restlessly in his sleep. He coughed again. Sissie heard it. The match box and the lighted stick fell from Sissie's hands. She sat on the edge of the bed. After a second of being perfectly still, she moved with the greatest effort she must have ever made in her whole life, and brought her left foot on the glowing match. Then she threw herself back on the bed and burst into tears.

To end the news, these were the main headlines:

'President Reagan . . .'

Payments

Kumwa, did you say that behind all this *pah-pah* I am doing, I may be feeling bad inside? Shu-wa! Ah you, you know me well. Yes, I feel a little bad inside. But that is because I am that kind of a fool! . . . as for this one, let me too have my laugh. I would not be me if I had not spat on her. Sell that thing my fish? For an act like that, my soul would fly away in shame. Yes, I am glad. Even though I know my life is not going to change for the better now just because I spat into the eyes of a whore. What pains me a little is that I had chewed a stick at all in the morning. Because for her type, the best is to splash them all over with something from a mouth that is stale from a whole night's sleeping. But who knows, there may be a next time yet.

No one should get me wrong. I am not completely fearless. I too would rather be in my house sleeping, or at least thinking about my many problems, than fall into their hands for any reason at all. But there are things one's soul demands should be done. Like: can't I decide whom to sell my fish to? The fish I buy with my own money? The fish that I bargain for? And if there is only one person alive who wants to buy my fish and I don't like the idea of that person eating my fish, I say: can't I deny such a creature the pleasure of buying my fish so that she would have to look elsewhere for fish or then she simply does not have fish to eat at all today, tomorrow and the next? I choose my pride and also stay poor. Fools like me do things like that . . .

No, I did not sell her my fish. I spat on her instead. But God, thinking of people and how foolish they can get makes me pity them. Look at the lot of you. If there was nothing wrong with you all, how could you tell me that I cannot refuse to sell my fish to a customer I hate? Because this is exactly what I have just done. And nothing has happened to me? I have not yet started foaming on the mouth? Or dropped dead?

So what, even if I drop dead? I would still have done the one thing that I had badly wanted to do: and that, my sisters, is something that does not happen to some of us everyday. What surprises me about people is how they can go around saying we must not do this and we must not do that, even though 'this' and 'that' are probably the only one or two things left that we can do. What I am saying is that the things we really cannot do anymore are so many that we only destroy ourselves even more by fearing to do some of the one or two things left which we can still do . . .

As for the story, I have already told it to so many people who do not have the wits to understand, now I am weary with the telling of it. Words too are only air while what happens inside of us is solid. Yet even if people were not so stupid, it still would have been difficult for me to make any words say fully to them what my feelings are on this matter.

Hei, Esi Bo, don't ask me to stop carrying on as if things that happen to me had never happened to humans before. Who are humans? What kind of animals are they? I don't know, maybe you do. All I know is that even down there under my foot, I still hurt if I step on a thorn. Yes, after all the walking-walking I have done here-under-the sun, and with my soles gone harder than the back of a crocodile.

Esi Bo, you are looking at me sleepy-eyed? Which means you do not understand what I am saying? So then, how is it you come talking to me, Ekuwa Esuon, in proverbs? I know a few too, my sister, and what I am telling you is that 'to her who

106

never is hurt by that which is painful, painful things never stop happening.'

Maybe worse have happened to mankind. But I hurt in a special way. And how can I not when even my marriage has been spoilt? Listen, I am not one of these silly women who would sit in the shade of an afternoon and regale their companions with stories of the doings between themselves and their men. Besides, my husband's problems are his own. I bring his name into this only because it is important for a woman in her dealings with the world, that her husband works or does not work.

I have always liked Tawia Mensa very much. But for a long time now, living with him has not been easy. And why? I shall soon tell you.

It was different before. When he was working at Akosombo. I don't know whether a thought which has just come into my mind is true. But ask any other woman who thinks she is also a human being in her own right and not just a flea feeding on a man. What I am saying is that it seemed to have been good for our marriage that we lived away from each other some of the time. Because when he came on visits, we were so busy bringing our heads together over our problems, we had little time for quarrels and fights. But since he lost his job, and came to live in the house, we have not stopped quarrelling. A man of muscle who has learnt his own trade cannot help feeling irritated when he cannot support himself.

No, he has not been sitting idle. How can you ask me that, Ekuwa, when you have been to my house several times and found him shaving wood or doing something like that? Now can anyone tell me how much a carpenter earns who lives among fishermen who themselves have got only leaky boats and broken nets? What new houses do they build? What spaces do they have that a carpenter can furnish? No, the people among whom we live have no jobs for Tawia Mensa to do. When someone dies, they order a coffin: and that of the cheapest kind. So that, after he has taken out the cost of the wood, what is left is just about what covers the nails and the varnish.

Do I then need to mention that I feed and cover up our buttocks with rags? Every morning and every afternoon, I have had to bring my tray here. Like all of you. My friends, I don't have to tell you that life is already difficult to live?

What are you saying, Adadewa? That 'even so, one cannot hate someone one does not know'?

Hah, you don't know. Call me all the names you like. Yes, I am spiteful, I am envious. I am still without shame, telling you that I hate bitterly, all the few women whose lives are so easy that they can never need anything. So much they have got! And my friends, you want to tell me that nothing pulls you in your stomach, never at all, when these women come swinging their arms, so fearful of the foul air around you, they won't even open their mouths to bargain for the price of your fish? So that no matter how much beyond the limits of honesty and decency you raised the price of your fish, they always have got the money to buy them, and more? As for me, when such a woman places herself in my hands, what else can I do but something to hurt her too a little?

Don't
You all swallow me up
With your cries of:
'Ekuwa Esuon, you are bad'
'Ekuwa Esuon, you are bad'.

Yes, I am bad. But it was the whore's own fault for coming to me in the first place. She could have chosen to come to any of you lot who delight in selling your wares to these ladies.

You say my soul should learn to delight in that which is beautiful or sweet?

Nonsense. Am I not a human being too? I can delight in anything sweet and good. And as much as any of you. What I cannot do is to delight in beauty and sweetness that someone else is enjoying. I have already told you that I know I am a fool. But then I am not the kind to sniff at the aroma from someone's fine soup, smack my lips and just continue sitting, while my bowels scream with hunger.

Now take the ladies that you daily flatter into buying your fish. I have seen them before. And I have certainly seen the like of that little tart before. Same car, black with glass that looks like it had been smoked, driven by the same driver when she came here to buy fish. She had the same hairstyle, the same bleached face and hands, the same lazy and insolent voice . . . Ah, but I am asking, fishwives of fishermen, do you know what happened to that one?

> Don't move, Ekuba. Don't run, Nkoso.
> Sit down and let me tell you something.
> They auctioned her stuff at the central market.
> Don't look at me like that. It is the truth I am telling you.
> Ask anybody. I may be as wicked as you say. But I do not
> fear any human being enough to want to tell a lie to.

They auctioned her wigs, her trinkets, dresses, shoes, bags and even *bodice* and *drawers*. It was an unbelievable heap, yet they auctioned them all. Including an elastic belt they say they make specially for ladies to hold their pads in place when they menstruate.

Yes.

The auctioneer was holding this elastic object up with a stick, while children who sell blades and old villagers who sell kenkey nudged at each other, asked what it was and giggled or exclaimed 'shame' at the answers they received.

Yes.

They sold everything of hers including what people said she herself had bought and preserved from the days when she was a petty trader, and before her school-teacher husband became a very big man in the government.

Yes, they sold everything: every little thing she possessed, while her relatives stood by with their hands on their heads and tears rushing down their cheeks waa, waa.

Me? Buy such rubbish? Not me. There must be bad luck in such clothes, even if they are sold for nothing. I do not need more ill-fortune in my life ... and why should I not laugh remembering? It was a good cine. I just watched my fill.

Do you wonder then that I found it so vexing that that girl who is only the new version of that older woman should come preening herself to me?

My sisters, call me names. Ashiale! My eyes do not blink at the glory of your ladies. And as for that one who came here this morning, I have encountered her before.

Yes, I mean herself.

When she was a nurse at the hospital. She had gawky ways and buck-teeth. Now they have removed the teeth and stuffed artificial ones into her mouth, straight and even. They have bleached her skin, put a wig on her head, and expensive clothes around her shoulders.

No, Ekuwa: don't ask me if what I am saying is true. I have already told you that I do not fear anyone to tell a lie to. But it should make sense that she walked through the whole lot of you and came to me? Indeed, thinking over it again, I would be surprised, if my face had not looked familiar to her at all.

It happened in connection with a serious illness my second

110

child had. You are right, Korankyebaa. It is sometime ago. It was a few weeks after the first government was overthrown. And as you may remember well, we were all so foolishly happy then. The child was not even one year old when the disease attacked her. A kind of difficulty with her breathing.

No, it was not asthma. Perhaps it was. But at the time, I was frightened . . . I could not have thought of asthma. And since then it has never seized her again. But as you know, asthma just does not disappear like that.

I took her to the hospital where they put her in bed. A few days later, Tawia Mensa arrived suddenly from Akosombo. With a story but no money. That as a result of the government being overthrown, work had been stopped on the big factory buildings they were building. He had had only a month's pay to look forward to. I asked him why? He himself did not know. They never explain to people like carpenters and painters why certain things should be done or not. Although it is a long time since the coup and when they were laid off, no one has troubled their heads thinking whether people like Tawia Mensa are still alive and if they ever eat.

I am not going to say that Tawia Mensa was a good husband then and now he is a bad one. But once upon a time, he was a working man. He was earning money. And also although one imagined quite a bit of this money was going to some lazy no-good bitch in Akosombo, ah, a man has his needs. Besides, even if what came monthly from him was not enough for us to feed on for a week, at least something always came with him whenever he was here to visit us. And he often sent a little something through the post office too.

So as I was saying, they put the child in a hospital bed and Tawia Mensa arrived with his story. So what else could I do, being a messenger of want? My friends, only my own death

111

could have prevented me from coming here to the boatyard for fish every morning and every afternoon. Yet the baby was still nursing and I had to be in the ward every time she was hungry.

Oh yes, my sisters. If your child has never been admitted into the children's ward of this central hospital, then rejoice. Because at least, that is one tribulation you have not suffered. I have heard that in expensive hospitals where people have got the money to pay more, the nurses are kinder. That they feed the babies on baby milk so that the mother does not have to be present all the time. But here? I used to leave home at five o'clock in the morning, wash my face and mouth, put on my cloth, go to the hospital, wash the child, feed it, get here to buy what leftovers the boys who hang around the boats had to sell, which I often discovered was going bad anyway, and was only good enough for curing, which means having to take a *tro-tro* to Anaafo. I hurried to the food market to buy one or two items, took them home, fed my first child and then rushed back to the hospital to feed the baby at midday, after which, I took the Municipal bus and hurried back here, in the early afternoon, bought fish, sold them, then went back home to wash up and hurry to catch the bus to the hospital to prepare the baby and feed it for the night.

Yes. Yes. Yes, my sister.

This is what life was for me, for days and days and days.

It was always very late in the day when I remembered that Tawia Mensa was living with us and he too was in need of comforting and some plain food. You don't have to get me to tell you that a man can behave strangely about his food. Or shall I just say that the way a man behaves about his woman's cooking shows how he feels about her? Tawia Mensa lost his appetite for my cooking then, and has never really got it back since.

I was very late going to the hospital one evening. As I hurried along the corridor, so anxious to get to my child, I met the mother of another sick baby, as she was leaving the children's ward. She told me that my child was crying. And that she had been crying for a long time. I didn't hear what else she had said or wanted to say. I just flew towards the entrance to the ward. But then, as soon as the nurses saw me, they shut the door to the ward and although I begged and begged, they refused to let me go in to my crying baby. Instead, they began heaping insults on me, and accusing me of things in my life which, if they had been true, those nurses would certainly not have known of, being strangers.

What did I say back? Nothing. What could I say? You don't hit anyone on the head if your fingers are in her mouth, do you? I was beginning to hope after a while, that some of them thought they had washed me clean enough with their mouths and were ready to let me go to my baby. But for this lady that was here a little while ago.

Yes, my sisters. It is true what they say. God creates every person and his enemy in the same minute.

I had never met this girl before. Yet, the way she refused to let me go to my baby when it was crying all that time, you would have thought she was paying me back for some evil I had already done her.

But the baby cried for the rest of the evening and much of the night.

How could I go home? Or sleep?

Listen, if your child is lying in that hospital and you want to sleep there at nights to be on hand should the child need you, it is very little sleep you get anyway; because you have to sleep on the bare cement floor; unless you bring a reed mat from your house. Besides, some child is crying nearly all the time. If it is not your child, it is sure to be somebody else's.

But then my ears were on my baby the whole night. When its

poor lungs could not support any more loud crying, she stopped and just whimpered. In fact, at some point, that she-devil's workmates began to beg her to let me in. I could hear them and understand when they stopped speaking the whiteman's language and talked in our own.

No, I did not know whether she was senior to all of them or not. I have asked myself many times since . . . No, I was too blind with anxiety to notice what colour of uniform she was wearing.

In the morning, they let me in with the other mothers. The baby's breathing had become even more difficult. After washing it, I thought I would feed it, but it refused to take my breasts.

No, it was not at all possible for me to go home that morning.

I therefore decided to wait around until the doctor came to the ward so I could tell her what had happened. But soon I realized what a fool I was. The night-nurses left and the morning-nurses came. I tried to get the witch's name by describing what I thought I remembered of her. But they looked at me with vacant unknowing eyes as if I was talking in my sleep. Later, I learned that even if I had been able to identify her, there would have been no use to it. They say no doctor likes to make noises about such happenings because it gives their work a bad name.

Hmm. Yes, what nonsense, Adadewa. Don't be wise on me. Just think. What does it matter even if it is not the same person? Yes, maybe she just looked like the other girl. But don't you think that that in itself is enough to make me want to do something terrible to her: even without her opening her mouth to ask me anything?

Ah, yes. I am sure too that many people have died other people's deaths because of resemblances. Sorry to their ghosts.

In this case though, I am sure that was her. And after what she did to me, she comes asking me for the price of a whole basketful of fish, and on being told the price, goes on to ask me if they were fresh because she was not going to sell them but eat them. Taking me for a half-wit too, eh? Couldn't she have realized that someone like me knows that no woman comes to the fishmarket to buy fish to go and sell, dressed as she was? And sitting at the back of a very big car? But she had to take special care to let me know that she is buying scores of huge soles just to go and eat them in her house. My God, today? Today? When to afford a single dried-out herring is a problem for many?

Don't say 'Hmm'. Just tell me: Who are these ladies? How were they born? What did God specially bless them with? What did He put between their legs?

Or how can a woman tell another woman she is buying a big basketful of some very precious fish just to take home to eat? No, my sisters, I have spat on her. And I will again if she comes back asking me questions. I am very sure she is the same person who rejoiced to see my child suffer. But then, they are all the same, these your ladies whom you flatter daily to buy your fish.

True, they have got the money. But so what? You, my sister, you behave just like fishmongers.

When you are selling fish, you refuse to do anything else but sell fish. Whereas I, Ekuwa Esuon, I sell my fish and look around too.

Oh yes, you are right.

What I see cannot make me happier. Life is full of horrors. But I allow myself a good stare.

Ah, thinking of what I was feeling when the whore was standing in front of me, she should be thankful to her God that she has escaped with her neck.

Eh, what are you saying?

That her man is the most important man of the region and therefore they are coming to arrest me? For spitting on her? And

115

that for this crime, they can come and take me to Ankaful prison or the mad house? Let them. It's all part of the wear and tear that is life. If I don't fight my battles now, who would fight them for me, and when?

Male-ing Names in the Sun

Toli* Number One

In May 1949, a young girl stood in the blazing sun on the parade grounds of Dominase, the district capital of Abeadze in the south central region of a country then known as the Gold Coast. She and her schoolmates had been there for at least two hours, waiting for they-didn't-know-whom-but-the-then District Education Officer to come and inspect them. The inspection was part of the main business of the day. The girl had led her school's contingent (in a two-file formation) that marched for four kilometres between their village and the parade grounds.

The early morning excitement of dressing up for the occasion had died down, although if you had asked the girl and her companions, they would not have confessed to the fatigue, hunger and thirst. And why should they, when they were the chosen few from the whole district? Earlier, they had stood stiffly at attention. Now they were chattering to one another, now squatting, now straightening up, or just generally fidgeting. One or two bold individuals were testing the teachers' patience by breaking free from their own positions to run between the lines.

It was 'Empire Day', the name given to the birthday of a certain English woman called Victoria Alexandrina. The girl

* Toli is the pidgin for a story. The term is often used to mean 'a tall tale'.

117

was to learn later that this Victoria had been 'the Queen of the United Kingdom of Great Britain and Ireland', and strangely, also 'the Empress of India'. Victoria, alias Mrs Albert Francis Augustus Emmanuel of Saxe-Coburg-Gotha, had been born over one hundred years before this African child was born, and died in the second year of the 20th century.

What she was to remember most clearly from the day though, was that she had wanted to scratch her right palm very badly. She had also been aware that she should not. She had been told that as a hyperactive toddler, she had sustained a big and vicious burn when she stumbled, fell and put her palm solidly in the middle of a wood fire on which her mother was cooking. This scar, she had been warned, would itch whenever she felt hot and uncomfortable . . .

It is a fact that in the south central region of Ghana, there is a division of the Akan nation known as the Fanti. It is also a fact that until quite recently, *Fanti* was an entry in nearly all respectable and scholarly dictionaries of the English language, including those reprinted in the 1960s. The user was informed that as an adjective, 'fanti' as in to go *fanti* meant to 'go native' (sic), 'wild', 'untamed' . . . The girl's first language was Fanti.

Nobody spoke well of the Fanti as imperial subjects: and that included Fantis themselves. While the British lamented that 'those damned Fantis' were ungovernable, the Fantis unashamedly boasted of their recalcitrance, their rudeness, their contempt for the imperial set-up, and for the whiteman. Their language was crammed with proverbs and other sayings attesting to this.

'*Aban wotwiw n'adze, wonsoa n'* .'
You don't carry a government (on your head). You drag it behind you.

118

'*Kohwinyi na ose ne dasefo wo Aborokyir.*'
It is a liar who claims his only witness is in Europe. (Who wants to go that far to bring such a witness?)

Fantis called every whiteman '*Kwesi Buronyi*'. 'Kwesi' is a Sunday-born male. And why? Whitemen = missionaries = Christians = Sunday's children (or Sunday workers). '*Buronyi*' is 'corn person'. That is, 'one with cornsilk hair'. There was no equivalent nickname for white women. Maybe they did not exist in the imagination of Fantis.

The girl also grew up knowing that long before she was born, her grandfather had been arrested along with other '*Nkwakwafo*'* for 'disturbing the King's peace'. They had been sent to the castle prison at Elmina, and tortured. The mode of torture was to force the prisoners to pass cannonballs among themselves, as though they were playing volleyball. Within a week, they were dead, each and every one of them, including her grandfather. No beatings, no bruising. Very gentlemanly, very civilized.

By the way, the fact that these days, our governments are post-colonially (!) torturing and killing Africans does not lessen or justify colonial crimes. It only goes to show how long our people have suffered.

God say, God say, God say
God say, God say, God say
God say, God say . . .
God say, God say, God say
God say, God say, God say
God say, God say, God say
God save the King . . .

* This term means 'youngmen', and refers to a specific group within the Akan socio-political structure.

119

Ghanaians never sang the lyrics of the British anthem as they were taught, instructed and were expected to. Not if they could help it. Of course, much of the time, most of them could. But why should they sing that anthem correctly? It was too much trouble. 'After all, it isn't our mother's anthem,' is what they would have probably told anyone if challenged. Nothing concerning the empire was their mother's or their father's. So they took their time to do everything; they did everything half-heartedly or they didn't do anything at all.

Ghanaians have always suspected that Kwame Nkrumah influenced the choice of May 25th as Africa Day. (Also known as 'OAU Day', or 'Africa Liberation Day'.) The 24th of May had been Empire Day. You do not have to take someone's 'day' over. You only put yours close enough for people to remember 'the good old days', without considering the change spiteful.

These days, Empire Day is supposed to be Commonwealth Day. Commonwealth Day? So you ask yourself what on earth you've got to do with Boris Yeltsin? You wonder if it refers to Yeltsin's or Lenin's birthday? However, you also suspect that if there is a Russian whose birthday ought to be celebrated by someone, it should be Vladimir Ilich Lenin because in his heyday, he was revered by as many people as Victoria had been in hers. Whiteman's tribal politics. All this business of the mind of the African child getting farmed out to different European centres of power was always quite tragic really. It's like suffering from a permanent migraine. No wonder we are amnesiac. Meanwhile everyone expects us, and we expect ourselves, to solve all our problems instantly. Whew!

So then was W. E. B. Dubois some malevolent wizard cursing humankind into stupidity and intolerance when he said that the problem of the 20th century was going to be that of race? Or was he just an honest prophet? One thing is certain. Seventy years after he spoke and with only a few years of the century left, the issue of race is still allowed to assume all forms, subsume all controversies and consume every little bit of human energy, vision and imagination. The 21st century is almost upon us, and we are still imprisoned in the colours of our skins.

How absolutely awful! How humanly pathetic!

When we are going about our normal business, we do not stop to wonder whether we might have experienced the whole imperial/colonial *wahala* differently if we had been white? However, on some idle occasions, we do wonder. Of course, the honest answer is a clear 'yes'. After all, we were 'the natives' whose lands and other resources had to be taken and given to the emperor's relatives in Australia, Canada, Kenya and Zimbabwe, no? Why some of them had to leave their homes became irrelevant once they arrived in our neighbourhoods.

God say, God say, God say
God save the King . . .

Toli Number Two

A FRAGMENT FROM A LOST NOVEL

Once upon a time, there was a fisherman who lived in Mowure, a seaside village in the Central Region. As everyone who knows the area is aware, Mowure is really within a stone's throw from the town of Oguaa . . . ahh-h . . . First, about Oguaa, alias Cape Coast.

Those were the 1920s. Oguaa was the big city of the Fantis,

121

who were then congratulating themselves for having used (read 'helped') the British to conquer the Ashanti, their more aggress- ive relatives to the north, of whom they were always in mortal fear. The British had 'pacified' Ashanti, looting Kumasi the capital, especially of its legendary gold arts, and finally exiling the king and other core members of the royal family. Other feats the Fantis had recently accomplished included making Oguaa unviable as the seat of the colonial government.

Now Oguaa was settling down to become the self-appointed, self-conscious fashion centre of the Gold Coast, while its people set about the business of Europeanizing themselves with panache. In dressing, they opted for the clothes of the owners of the Empire, as the latter dressed in their cold country. So under the 88 degree sun, the men wore three-piece *woollen* suits, complete with top hats. The women wore the equivalent long evening gowns, hats, together with stockinged feet, gloved arms and hands and all.

According to the rest of the country which came to look upon their antics with a mixture of derision and envy, this was also when Fanti wives started the *haute cuisine*, that became so *haute*, it tipped over into requiring women to light their charcoal and wood fires with butter, and at the end of a cooking session, to extinguish the fires with milk. And that in a region of the world where there had never been dairy farming at all. In fact, one cow seen within a 20-kilometre radius was a spectacle enough for people to name their children after, and for the day to be remembered in historical narratives. So both the milk and the butter were tinned and imported from England, or the Netherlands . . .

Maybe, it's time to return to the fisherman . . .

He had been the only surviving child from his mother's six full-term pregnancies. So as an Ewuewu, Abiku or a Kwasamba, and in line with custom, his parents had had to give him a name

122

he would not have wanted to return to his spirit mother with. They chose Srako, the local term for One Shilling. Since he was born on a Wednesday, his full name was Kweku Srako, although everybody conveniently forgot the Kweku and just called him Srako. Srako and his wife had eight children in all, and thereby proved more fertile than his parents. Their fourth born but first son was Kojo Kuma, named after a revered ancestor of his father's house.

One day, just as Srako was setting out to sea, his wife Esi-Yaa asked him to listen to a thought that had occurred to her. 'What is it?' he had asked somewhat impatiently, standing. 'Sit down,' she commanded. Srako could not believe his ears. Was the woman going out of her mind? As if it was not provocation enough to bother him with woman thoughts when he should be on his way. However, he was also thinking that the surest way to bring bad luck on himself and his mates would be to quarrel with any woman now. He sat down. She sat opposite him.

'Y-e-s?'

'We should send Kojo Kuma to school,' Esi-Yaa said firmly.

'*Nyankopon*-above and the Gods of our Fathers!' he exclaimed as he jumped up, fetched his sack and dashed out to go and join his mates who were by then taking the dragnet to their boat.

Srako could not believe that he had heard Esi-Yaa right. How could the same idea occur to him and to her? When a few days earlier, he had realized he should send Kuma to school, he had postponed discussing it with her because he was not sure of how she would react. (Meaning, he had not convinced himself that it was a good idea.) After all, as their oldest son, the child would be expected to go to sea, and in fact, very soon. He was about ten years old. Besides, sending him to school would mean exiling him to go and stay with some of those snobbish and cruel Cape Coast characters. He had decided to give the matter

123

a think-over while he was at sea on this trip. Now he would forever have to give the woman the credit of being the first in bringing up the matter. Ah, ah, ah!

A month later, Srako, his wife Esi-Yaa and their son Kojo Kuma were on their way to Oguaa. It had to be a Tuesday, since that is the sacred day of Nana Bosompo, the god of the sea, and a day on which no self-respecting fisherman would go to sea. A hol(y) day. They set out quite early. By the time the sun was shaking itself up to be hot, they were on the eastern outskirts of the town. Around half-past eight, they knocked on the door of Isaac Goodful, the circuit minister of the Methodist Church.

Going to the priest instead of any of the Oguaa residents was not the result of a random decision made by Srako. Apart from being the immediate leader of his church, the priest was also some kind of a distant relative. Meanwhile, not wanting to take any chances, he had sent a message to the priest to please expect them. Soon Srako, his wife Esi-Yaa, Reverend Goodful and his wife 'Maame Sofo' Mrs Goodful were seated around a big table. The boy had been deposited with the priest's 'boys' somewhere in the back of the house. The discussion was short and concluded soon enough. Or almost. It was agreed that Kojo Kuma would stay with Osofo and his wife, as one of about half a dozen youngsters, apart from their own children, who lived in the priestly household, getting properly brought up and educated.

Kojo Kuma was sent for. He came and stood before the priest, with his cloth neatly wrapped around his body, and the upper ends tied behind his neck. The presence of his parents gave him some courage, but he was still shaking. The priest looked completely formidable. Even seated, he was much taller than the boy on his feet.

'What is your name?'

'Kojo.'

'Kojo what?'

'Kojo Kuma.'

'I hear you want to go to school?'

Kojo nearly said that actually, it was his parents' idea. He liked the thought of it, anyway. So he nodded. The four grown-ups jumped on him.

'Hei, that's not done.'

'You cannot use your head to answer a question.'

'You must open your mouth and say: "Please Master, yes." '

The last was from Srako. As for the boy, all he wanted to open his mouth to do was cry. But if he did, everybody would shout at him. That 'a man does not cry.'

'Kojo,' the priest began again, kindly. 'What is your Christian name?'

'Osofo, we have not baptized him yet,' Esi-Yaa cut in.

'So you had not thought of a Christian name?'

'Osofo, no.'

'I can baptize him even this coming Sunday. But we must find him a Christian name.' He paused significantly. Then: 'We shall call him George,' he said with finality.

As we are all supposed to know, 'George' is nowhere in the Bible. It just happens to be one of the names often given to the men who sit on the throne of England.

'Osofo, we thank you,' Srako and his wife said in unison.

'Thank you, Osofo,' Kojo Kuma piped after his parents.

'Next time, you must say, Sir . . . Thank you, Sir.'

Another pause. 'The child must also have a surname,' the priest pressed on, addressing the parents.

Hardly finding his voice, Srako asked, 'Osofo, what is a surname?'

The man of God chuckled to himself. He cleared his throat, faced the fisherman squarely and explained that 'surname' really meant 'sire's name', a name which you get from your father.

'Kuma ... Kojo Kuma,' the fisherman timidly intervened.

'Ow,' said the priest, 'but that is the boy's *own* name, no?'

'Yes,' the mother, the father and the son had all replied. Then Srako added clearly, '*I* gave it to him. He was named after his great grandfather, my father's father.'

The Reverend had tried to be patient, but all this was taking too long, and getting too far. How could he explain the new system brought by the Europeans to them? He knew that his people's naming system defined each individual clearly, with no ambiguities. However ... but then ... yes, he had to admit it to himself, it was based on some ... eh ... unfortunately primitive combination of both patrilineal and matrilineal notions. Whereas the European system of naming people against one singular male line was ... eh ... more ... sensible, Christian and civilized.

His guests watched his face with anxiety. He would have to explain it to them some other time. Maybe, he could even build a sermon around it, since the question was probably cropping up all over, as people took advantage of the new order and enrolled their children in the whiteman's schools. This morning though, he didn't have much time. So barely able to conceal his impatience, he told them that the law from the Europeans said that when children go to school, they must have their father's names as their surnames. So the boy's surname was Srako, and he would be registered in school as George Srako.

Another pause. Something had occurred to the priest. Srako is Shilling! He exclaimed into the air. 'Kojo, your name is George Shilling! ... No, since it's your father's name, and you are the son of Shilling ... Kojo, your name is Shillingson. George Kojo Shillingson.'

G. K. Shillingson!

G. K. ... G. K. ... G. K. ... The priest was very excited. How could he help it? He had just remembered that he had heard there was a distinguished Englishman called G. K. Chesterton. What he was not sure of was what this other G. K. was distinguished for ...

In time, G. K. Shillingson became a distinguished lawyer. He had many children with his lawful Christian wife, Mrs Docia Shillingson, as well as other women: including his receptionist; a young girl from the 'hinterland' who was a servant in his house; and at least one hawker he had lured to his offices. That was to half explain the different kinds of spellings of the name which were passed down over the years.

People also point out that over the years and as an educated, westernized, civilized and self-consciously developing patriarchy, the Shillingsons spread their male seeds in the countries of Europe. Where, failing to blend their skins into their new environments no matter how hard they tried, they laboured to at least get the family name to conform to that continent's different tribal ways of spelling.

And so, in time, apart from the original SHILLINGSON, there were SHILLINSONS, SHELLINGSONS and SHILILLNSTONS, SHILLINSSONS, SHILLINSSENS, SCHILLENSOHNS, SCHIELLINSOHNS, SCHILLEINSENS, SCHILLIGSENS, SCHILLENSTEINS and ZWILLENSENS ... They even say that when some got behind the then Iron Curtain – of course, some did! – they became either ZWILLENVITZ, ZVILENSKY or CZVILLENYEV.

Toli Number 3

This is May 1992. We hear that a couple of days ago, something interesting happened in Oguaa. A young woman called Achinba was getting married to Dr Kwesi Shillingson. They even say that she is the granddaughter of the little girl who stood in the sun on Empire Day. We also hear that when everything was ready for the wedding, her future mother-in-law called her to her inner chamber to talk to her, woman to woman. That Mrs Bessie Shillingson had made the mistake of opening the meeting with, 'My Lady, as a future Mrs Shillingson . . .'

'Maa, I shall not call myself Mrs Shillingson,' Achinba declared.

'Ei,' Mrs Bessie thought she had not heard right. 'You mean you are not going to marry my son?' 'I am,' Achinba giggled and then continued: 'I am marrying Kwesi. But I want to keep my own name . . . I like my name. Besides, you know that as a professional woman, an architect, everybody knows me as Achinba . . .'

They say that Achinba need not have bitten back what she was about to say next but had thought better of. Which was that she loved her man, but not his name . . . because she had always thought Shillingson sounded funny, and silly . . . They say that in fact Achinba could have said all that and more to Mrs Bessie. No one would have heard her. Because Mrs Bessie had decided to faint a long time ago. You know the kind of fainting spells certain women suffer when they do not want to hear, or otherwise deal with, anything unpleasant? . . . This kind of fainting, her own son, the doctor, was later to admit privately to himself, was an art: an art perfected in Europe by the mothers and the wives of the men who built the Empire.

Newly-Opened Doors . . .

. . . that's what the politician who represented our district those first days of Independence said we were going to get. Our lives were going to be full of them: newly opened doors, 'now that the whites are leaving.'

And the whites. Were they really leaving? Not those I knew. Oh yes: one or two, maybe. In any case, we were to discover soon enough, that that was not even our real problem. Our real problems had very little to do with whether the whites left or not. No, that is not true. I mean, the whites leaving or not leaving being a problem or not being a problem. What I'm trying to say is that whether the whites stayed or left was a problem. But it was only a little problem which was part of a big problem which had nothing to do with them.

My sister, you think it all sounds very confusing? I agree with you. Hm, this life can be very funny. My sister, do you remember how clear everything was before Independence?

Nothing was confusing then. The world was divided into: us and those white people. They had come and conquered our ancestors: shot, hanged and in other unspeakable ways killed off multitudes. Those who survived had had their lives but nothing else. The whites had taken their lands, leaving our ancestors sitting on rocks with their bare buttocks or working as slaves – no one called it that then though – in their fields and in their homes. That's how things were, and how they would have stayed till the end

129

of time. If we had not fought them. But we fought them. Lord, how we fought the whites! We went ourselves or sent off our children. Those of us who stayed out there came back without eyes, hands and legs. We returned home, leaving bits and pieces of our flesh in the woods. Can you imagine? Eyes, ears, hands and legs . . . one or two or all of them . . . and sometimes, minds even. As far as I knew, we were fighting to drive the whites out of our land. Simple. Nothing at all confusing about that.

And now suddenly, nothing is clear-cut anymore.

Yes, Mande. My mind was somewhere else. No, it was in another time . . . I am sorry. So was yours? . . . Hm, as I was saying, now everything is confusing. Everything has been confusing for a long time . . . maybe from the beginning . . . For one, when the white farmer my father used to work for was leaving, he sold . . . sold?! . . . Yes, we heard he had sold his farm to the government for a lot of money. Then later, we heard that the man who represented our district had bought the same farm, the same land, all of it, for less than what the government had paid the whiteman for it . . . Wait, wait, wait, Mande, of course, I am not making sense. But how can I? How can any teller of a story make sense out of a tale that itself has no sense?

I should get on with my story? Well, which one? . . . Don't you dare tell me it's a sign of old age. And watch your mouth. Because if I am old, then you are not an infant yourself. After all, you are only about two years behind me.

As you know already, I have been a housegirl all my life. I thought I had seen all that there was to see in this lifetime, doing that kind of work. Both inside those homes I worked in and outside.

Ah, Mande, you are bad. You always want to hear me say it.

That what I never got used to about the job was the master or mistress calling me to bring something in or to take something out of a room when there were two of them in there, in bed, doing things to their bodies . . . and later, calling me to go in to take the towels from the bed when their body water was all over the place not yet dry . . . When I was younger, it did not bother me.

Huh, what did you say? . . . Mande, if you were not my sister, I would kill you.

Hm . . . But you are right. When you are too young for your body to have desires, it doesn't matter what you see others doing. Oh, but later . . .

And that is why this matter pained me so much. My sister, you can talk. You are so right. At my age, I should not put myself in situations where people will humiliate me. But what else could I have done? What else can I do? We pray for life. We pray for health. Whether by pouring libation to the ancestors or kneeling in church; because having life and health is wonderful. But it is not the end of the matter. We have to eat to stay alive and strong. And that takes money . . . and do I have to tell you that to get money we have to work?

Yes . . . oh yes . . . and no, oh no, I never thought that I shall have to be a servant for such a long time, and that even after the war some of us will be cleaning other people's homes. A war in which I lost two sons . . . You lost your only child? . . . A war which made my daughter mad . . .

What happened? Oh, Mande, but you know. I have told you about all this so many times. I sent you so many messages. I also remember writing you a letter.

You never got it? Shame. Anyway, I think you just don't want to remember. Because the last time you were home, I remember us telling you about all these things even then. Now, if this kind of wilful forgetfulness is not a sign of old age, I don't know what is. Of course, we are still teasing one another, thank God we still can. What will happen to us if we stopped laughing?

Now listen for the last time. Towards the end of the war, and you know things were really bad then? . . . Well, something terrible, something unspeakable, something really horrible happened to Rufa and her husband. You remember hearing about the death? Maybe that was the only really good thing he got out of that incident . . .

Why shouldn't I say that? It is the truth. I was never sure of what he had done exactly. But one side said they had proof that he was a traitor. Four men went to take him and Rufa one night to one of their camps. Once they got there, first they forced him to watch while they took turns raping Rufa. Then they put a machete in her hand and asked her to cut his head off. It took a long time. And to make sure she would not stop, they were cutting off one of her ears, bit by bit . . . When we found her, she was almost dead. Later, she recovered enough to tell the story, then she fell completely mute. As you know, she has not said a word in ten years . . . and everyday of our lives since then, I have had to get people help me force food into her mouth . . .

Mande, you and I know these stories too well. And we should stop reminding ourselves of our grief . . .

Okay . . . okay . . . you are right again. It is evening, it is raining outside and we have raked together some cents to go and buy this bottle of Belly Burner . . . Now who is not admitting how lucky we are, hm?

But as I was telling you . . .

Of course, that is the real story . . .

You know that when freedom first came I tried to get a proper job. I tried everything. Because I thought that with freedom, I could do something other than being a housegirl. After all, I had

132

passed my junior matric . . . I still have my certificate, framed. I tried everything. I told my ward secretary. I went to the offices of the New Women's Council. I also tried to see the man who was then our district representative at the regional assembly. I went to his office many, many times. Once I even went to his home. But home or office, they always told me he was not in. I was so determined to get a proper job that I also went to my grandchildren's school to see the people in the office. To tell them that if any of their cleaners left the job for any reason, I was interested . . .

My grandchildren? Of course, they lived with me. They still live with me . . . Mande, really . . . who else did you think would look after them when their mother can't do anything for herself? . . . You had refused to stay in this country because you said there was nothing here you wanted since your child never came back from the war. And I understand you well . . . But then, who else did I have to fall on? . . .

No, don't be funny. I am not bitter. At least, not until yesterday.

What happened yesterday? Eh . . . eh . . . why don't you just wait? . . . As I was saying, . . . yes . . . yes . . . I still look after three or four generations . . . our mother and father, myself and my husband, my daughter and her children . . . The children? There are three. You only remember Rose? That's because she was the first, and she was born already before you went into exile . . . in fact, even the second one was a tiny baby then. No, it is not strange if you can't remember her or the last one who was born when you were definitely out of the country. He was not even a year old when all that happened to his mother and father . . .

But oh no, I am not at all bitter. The truth is, I don't know any woman or man of our age here who is not living this impossible life. If they are well into their 50s, then they are looking after lots of people of different generations. If they are not, then they are dead, or by some chance, somebody else is looking after them . . . That was why I was so happy when Rose finished well in school and got one of the scholarships . . . Of course, the cost of all those books plus her pocket money is another tale . . . A-h-h-h . . . the strike. I have been very, very worried. Besides, just being home all the time is not good for anybody. But you listen to all the talk, and nothing seems to make sense to anybody except perhaps the Good Lord Himself. It is not at all clear who is right. Is it the students? The government? The teachers? . . .

Wait, I am coming back to the story. Except that now I don't think that there is much to it. For the past fifteen years, like I said, I was looking for a proper job. I mean a job working in an office. For the government or maybe some private company . . . but in an office. Because in these households, you never grow up.

At least, in an office, you can get promotion to something like Senior Cleaner. And sometimes, I hear there can even be a pension. Listen, don't you dare laugh at me. I know that in a few years, I shall be sixty, and therefore I don't have that much time to work towards a proper pension. What does it matter? I hear in government service, there is always gratuity . . . and anyway, with a job cleaning government offices, one day when I can no longer work, I can say that I too 'retired from the Civil Service'!

Yes, you heard right. I finally got an office job . . . with the government. So why am I acting like my world has just fallen apart? Well, my world has fallen apart . . .

Wait, wait, w-a-i-t. Wait and listen. I started only yesterday. I'm with the team that does the Ministry for Discussions and Other Things Like New Job Creation. I am the oldest on the team and the rest are a whole lot younger than me. So they call

134

me Ambuya, Mama, Ole Lady . . . whatever. They decided to give me the rooms of the top men, including those of the 'Chief' as they call such people these days. Maybe it was to welcome me or as a sign of respect or maybe that was where the person I am replacing used to work. They are on the first floor.

I don't know . . . It looked like everything was going to be fine . . . I also don't know whether whoever told me that I should do the cleaning after 6 in the evening made a mistake or not. The first time I went there, I found all the doors of that wing of the Ministry open, with lights on all over the place. So I just entered, went through the office of the receptionist, then the public relations officer's place and right through the secretary's room and then into the Chief's office . . .

What do you mean, I didn't bother to knock? There was nothing to knock on. I said that all the doors were open, didn't I? Besides, I did not need anyone to tell me that in such a place, you start with the room of the biggest person . . . Yes, Mande, even his door was not closed. That door too was open. So I just entered the room. And then I nearly fainted.

Right on a couch somewhere near the centre of the room, there was this man on top of a woman! . . .

Yes, right there. Don't ask me what I did. What could I do? The thing is, I was so shocked, I couldn't find any legs to run on. It was as if someone had nailed my feet to the ground. I stood there with my mouth open, my mind whirling. Meanwhile, he was not even pretending that my being there meant anything at all. I felt so ashamed. Then he screamed at me: to go away or something that sounded like that.

That was what freed my feet. I found myself running, running, running. Down the steps and you know what? All the time I was running, all I could think about were all those open doors. So many open doors. Why were there so many open doors? Why?

Nowhere Cool

Kinna   (*of five years old*): *Mama, Mama, why do you look so
         quiet?*
AAA: *Hmm . . . I am thinking*
Kinna: *Are you thinking again?*
AAA: *Yes.*
Kinna: *Mama, do people have to think all the time?*
AAA: *Yes, child, it looks like we have to. All the time!*

There were areas in our secondary school education at home that
I could never understand or cope with. Like English Literature.
While the sun blazed outside the classrooms, its heat strong
enough to warm great grandmother's bath water, we read about
carriages getting stuck in the snow. All that always made me feel
sleepy. But I didn't dare sleep. So I would just sit like a stone, my
eyes wide open but staring at nothing, while my thoughts wandered around familiar things that were being chased away by the
demands of the culture of our conquerors . . .

  'A penny for your thoughts, Sarah.' That was the voice of
Miss Jones. The command always achieved its intended effect. I
was jolted awake and my mind returned to the classroom and
mad women locked away in cold attics. 'A penny for my
thoughts?' I have always wondered why. Why would anyone
want another person's thoughts for a penny? Surely, there can
never be moderately-priced thoughts? Since our thoughts are
either so useless they aren't worth anyone else's dime, or they
are so precious, we wouldn't want to sell them for anything at
all?

She would always remember the jokes her male colleagues loved to tell about the position of women in traditional society. For instance, about how a man usually walked to the farm behind his wife: just in case there was danger ahead. 'With just a machete under his arm, while the woman carried the day's load on her head, and a child on her back . . .' A gender joke. Of course, like racial jokes, class jokes and other products of humour built on inner unpeace, the teller always hopes his listeners would take his ability to be so openly nasty as a sign of his freedom from privilege. Allah, how little we know ourselves as groups and how much less as individuals!

What she had come to learn is that being female has never been fun. Yes, ultimate pleasure is ours. But then, so is the last pain.

She knew she would always admit, and be grateful for, Kobla's support. The long hours of patient discussions they had had over their dilemmas. The concentration he had given to each possible solution that had presented itself.

'But there are workable compromises.' And Sissie sees clearly the face of her father relaxed, his whisky in hand after the morning service, on Sunday. Pensioned home from Eastern Nigeria where, for a native, he had been fairly senior in the colonial civil service, Papa certainly must have known about 'workable compromises'.

Meanwhile, there was the going itself. For three years. Away from Kobla . . . What a risk! 'These days, we are all so desperate, a sister would snatch up your man while you are away changing the baby's diaper.'

'Those forever unattached ones are a particular menace . . . Even decently married friends can be quite dangerous too . . .' said Bibi. Said Mariama.

Thinking of those two in particular, she realized with some shock that it was really true. They were always so quick to tell

137

her how lucky she was, married to Kobla, who was 'not only handsome, but you know, such a good conversationalist too, very different, research officer . . .' such things. Oh yes, they definitely made you feel that they would welcome a husband-swapping any day. Yet you would have thought that belonging already to the club of the saved was enough. So she couldn't help thinking too that there must be something in the belief that no human being is ever fully satisfied with her lot in life.

As for asking her mother-in-law to move in to look after the house, the children and Kobla, that too was another problem. 'Hei, it never works out.' Again, 'except for one or two blessed people. Much of the time, the old lady bustles around, cooking her son all his favourite dishes, while dropping a few hints here and there about how much better off she always knew he would have been with one of the simple unspoilt girls from the village . . .'

'My dear sister, there have been cases where the missus came back with her degrees and diplomas to find a brand new wife installed by the husband's family.'

'Nowhere cool, sister, ain't nowhere cool.'

Therefore, let me
hide here among
the thorns, while

I dine on wild desert grain
And if they should ask
you of me
tell them
the name of the game was
Life, and
I never learnt the rules.

Anyhow, to abandon her own life unlived: to say no to bits of good offers thrown in her way because taking them up might mean losing him, seemed plainly to her like a risky bet. 'And anyway, what woman has succeeded in holding a man who really wanted to go away from her . . .?'

'Aw, my mother's daughter, you are a child . . . Because when a man wants to go, he does. And it doesn't have to be another woman that takes him away from you. Anything can. Most things do. A man friend. A job. A car. Politics. Sports Te – le – vi – sion!'

'Say it and say it again, my child. You don't have to go swimming in the ocean to get drowned.'

'No, you can drown in your bath. They say it has happened to people with a pail of water in a bamboo outhouse! Otherwise would any devoted housewife who refused to go out of her house to work or play lose her man?'

What shook Sissie up was the thought of leaving the children for all that time. Two years definitely, possibly three. And the last-born under a year?

'Other women have done it.'
'Does that make it okay?'
And the horror tales are told:
Of children sent like cargo on strange airlines with their stranger hostesses. And the children arriving at airports to no relatives waiting because telegrams do not always arrive when we hope they would . . . phones do not always work . . . telex machines break down . . . 'And where some of us live, no one has heard of the fax yet! . . . Not always a bad sign . . . but . . .' Of children wasting away in towns and villages even though grannies spoil us so and aunties, uncles and daddy and mummy's friends treat us like their own that we are. But 'mother is gold and mother is silk: and

only an orphan finds comfort in the promise that if one
father is dead, there are several still living . . .'

Yet go she also knew she must. Pushed by so many forces
whose sources she could not fathom.

As the plane nosed its way up into the San-Something-or-
Other Valley across the immense American skies, she was doing
her best not to keep on thinking of home, when the quiet but
clearly exasperated voice broke into her consciousness:

'Please darling, sit still, please dear?'

She had to turn round and look. Of course, it came from just
the seat next to hers, a white woman and her two children, a
girl of about five years old and a baby of less than two, whose
sex was obviously of no interest to anybody yet; concealed as it
was under some unisex anybody-can-wear clothes. The baby
was straining across mother's lap to get to those skies, so
beautiful with the golden streaks of a day's ending. And it
couldn't have known that the window through which it wanted
to fly was permanently closed. Mother was having a hard time
stopping it though. And as if that was not enough, big sister
was scampering across the aisle and all over their section of the
plane touching other passengers and asking them questions.

Then the dinner came. Two trays. One for the mother,
one for the big girl, with some mushy-looking stuff for the
baby. Exasperation deepened on the mother's face. How on
earth was she going to manage? Soon they brought another for
Sissie.

Back home in Africa, the mother would have felt sure that
Sissie would want to help out. She would have dumped baby,
food and all on her neighbour's lap and expected her to feed the
child. And not just that. But love doing it too. Feel compli-
mented by the obligation! And here? Sissie decided to mind her
own business. Because for all she knew the woman was probably

feeling uncomfortable in her seat, on top of all her own troubles, because she was sitting next to a black person . . .

At the surprise party which Kobla had organized at some friends' for her – how had she managed to acquire this husband? – there had been quite a few speeches . . . How much we appear to want to say, especially when there is nothing much to say. Everyone had congratulated her on winning the fellowship award, and for the courage with which she had faced the prospect of leaving her husband and children behind.

No one had voiced out what she knew was in all their minds. That if the opportunity had come to Kobla, then he and all the wellwishers would have assumed that she would forget about her job, pack up the house, pack up the kids, and gone with him. It would have been so natural. Other women would have envied her. Yet there they were, telling her how brave she was, how brave some women can be . . .

It was almost the same at the cocktail party in New York. Her host family had met her at the JFK and driven her through a maze of streets to a hotel, one of several, east of what she was later to identify as Central Park. They had seen to it that all was somehow well there.

'You can't take too many chances: see, all black women ain't whores.'

Then they had suggested that she had better go straight to bed. 'You have to make up for the "jet lag".'

Jet-lag? What new beast is that? A peculiar disease of 20th century origin. Caused by flying, it attacks the central nervous system, effecting a disconnection between the mind and body. So that the patient spends several hours coaxing her mind to come and join her body from wherever she had originally boarded the plane to where she finally disembarked. Naturally, the longer the flight, the more serious the ailment.

In the evening, they had come to take her to the party. Quite a few people were there. Black black to white white with several shades in-between. Again later, she was able to identify the area as somewhere on Riverside Drive. She had set out determined to have fun. She was refreshed by the nap and excited at the prospect of unknown times ahead, masses of new people to meet.

She was never able to learn the name of who had thrown the party. Nobody else had seemed to know or care, anyway. But it had been a great evening. People dancing, drinking, smoking and openly touching as though they had just woken up to one another, and didn't expect this world to continue to exist beyond the next morning.

The party had gone on far into the night. No one had seemed over-anxious to go home, wherever that was. Instead, they had shown their tiredness by withdrawing into small groups. Again, as if everyone knew what the next phase should be. Eating, smoking, openly touching and now talking in exchange for dancing. So it was natural that she would find herself among a group of four young women. The sisters looked so charming and so roguish, their earlobes weighed down by unbelievably large earrings: circular, triangular, rectangular. And the sisters themselves, where had they come from? This round-faced Yoruba? That sloe-eyed Fulani? A long-limbed Kalenjin? And the black-lipped Wolof? And her heart warmed at the various beauty of a continent reflected unexpectedly, in a far-off-place. Her hand had gone up to her own head. She had known some embarrassment then . . . about her own straightened hair.

The sisters had rapped, suddenly serious because they had

142

learnt she was from 'The Mother Continent'. For until things are properly ironed out, pleasure, unalloyed pleasure for so many of us cannot ever last through any twenty-four-hour day ... They had asked her many questions. She had also asked them a few. Intimacy born as the morning broke. And by the lights of a brand new day, seeing the tallest buildings she had ever come across in all her life. Manhattan, New York.

Her new friends had looked a little tired and quite sleepy. But they couldn't get over the fact that she had left her children way out there on the other side of the Atlantic to come and study for two years or more. Wh-a-a-at! Each of them had been sure that in her place, they wouldn't have found the nerve. She in her turn had struggled to let them understand. That she was not different from anybody else. That no human being is born to be brave. We learn to be, when we are forced to.

'Yes,' agreed the sisters, who had then recalled some decisions of their own which they had found themselves making at some time or other to their own surprise. Not anything significant or earth-shaking. Like what their mothers had had to cope with. Or their grandmothers, on whom time and circumstances had forced harrowing painful choices.

'And consider this, huh, under slavery, black women, ... so many too ... not just an isolated case or two ... yeah ... it's said they had recipes passed down the generations ... so each woman knew it ... part of the business that prepared you for seeing your first blood ... Therefore, the choice was open to you from your early teens to menopause. G-a-a-a-d, what a hellishly long time too, to carry such a burden!' Oh, cosy private hell.

'So you mean?' asked Sissie with her English-as-a-Second-Language accent, which so many Americans were going to say

143

was charming. 'You mean they sometimes poisoned their own babies rather than . . . ?'

'Sure!'

'Or smother them in their cradle-sheets or choke them?'

'Sure!'

'Jesus.'

And of course, if you've seen a fatal accident before, no one needs tell you how frail we are at twenty, thirty . . . forty years. So how strong do you think anybody is, at a week, a day, a few hours old?

Just a belated abortion, and that's another very big issue. The mother must have managed. They always do or nearly always do. Yes, the mother must have managed. Sufficiently to have had time to say to Sissie:

'You sure you don't want to at least taste the food before they come for the tray?'

She had had to wake up and take note of the contents of the tray. She tasted a bit of this and a bit of that, and decided to keep the free 8 oz bottle of pink wine, provided to chic up the otherwise celluloid meal. As the trays were being removed, a voice came over the public address system, warning them of a few air-pockets ahead. They immediately tumbled into three in quick succession. The rest of the speaker's words trailed away in her own and other people's nervousness.

'Please darling, keep still. Please darling?'

This time, the little girl caught some fear from her mother's voice and started wailing as the plane kept lurching about, rather dangerously. Sissie drew up the midget curtains from the porthole and stared out. Grey and starless. Yet her watch read four o'clock. In the afternoon. Although she knew enough about changing seasons and their effects on daylight, she was still quite confused about time in this country where time changed from state to state. She put her watch to her ear and listened. She couldn't hear a thing. Reluctantly, she asked her neighbour for the time of the day.

'It's nine. But that's for New York. We are already in Southern California and it's only six o'clock here.'

'I see,' said Sissie, surprised and doubting.

'How can it be so dark outside then?'

'Sure? . . . mm . . . maybe we are going to get some rain.'

'We are meeting a storm, ladies and gentlemen,' a male voice full of strength came out on the address system. 'Please fasten your seat belts and put out all lighted cigarettes.'

A violent drop. A lurch. Thunder. Lightning. Can one actually hear raindrops pelting the roof of a plane? Or was it her imagination? The next few minutes were something else. No language or words can ever bring this type of experience to anyone. You go through it and know you've been there where life and death meet. Only other travellers who have also been to these zero points and returned know. Not necessarily on a plane flight. But also at some critical point in an illness or face to face with some other kinds of danger. A real beast as in lion, or some assailant on a lonely road: a weapon in hand, and eyes gleaming maniacally: hungry for sex, hungry for money that can buy food . . . Ave Maria, Holy Mother of God, and even the sign of the cross might not always save us . . . My brother, there is a special jet-age horror to suffer if you are encased in a plane that is floundering in space threatening any minute to crash.

'Please sweethearts, it should be all right in a little while.'

The baby had joined its sister, so that now the two of them were bawling their lungs out as though in another second, weeping would go straight out of fashion. Meanwhile, it was clear the noise of the crying children was not doing the nerves

145

of the people in their section of the plane any good. So they were turning their heads this way and that, with general discomfort and immediate disapproval. Sissie knew that like everybody else, there was nothing she could do but sit and wait.

She had never before taken time to contemplate what she would look like at her end. What she felt vaguely unhappy about was when she thought someone would dream of dolling her up in a blonde wig and some such fineries, the choosing of which would be done without her participation or approval. And now here, she was amused, as she contemplated her own lifeless body, lying there for people to come and gawk at ... Lord, any way you look at it, death is so undignified. But then luckily for air-crash victims, very often there isn't much of anything to put on view. Other funny images chased one another across her mind. And long after it was all over, she was to feel some shame that in actual fact, at no point during the crisis had she thought seriously about her children, their future and all that could have happened to them had the plane crashed among those alien mountains and she had died in it as everyone on board would most certainly have done.

'Excuse me, ma'm, but you wouldn't mind holding on to him while I calm her?'

She woke up suddenly, surprised. 'Oh, yes,' she said. So the little one was a boy?

'I am very sorry about the imposition but I can't cope alone.'

That was the mother again.

Sissie was already bending down to stand her bag on the floor to make room for the child. She noticed the top of its scalp first, like the centre of a circular crochet work or the base of a raffia basket. And she knew it was the closest she had ever got to the roots of a white head or indeed, of any non-African hair ... Kweli, what do you know? So many kinds of God's children ...

146

She saw the label then. In clear type and pinned on the crossroads of his braces, next to the centre of his backbone:

Allen Peters Jr
Aged 17 Months
c/o Allen Peters
36 Avenue de la Santa
Los Angeles 90022

She stared at the label and furtively touched it, to make sure it was really there. The typed card was inside a plastic casing, and attached to a small golden safety pin.

Cargo is cargo, live or dead . . .

She promptly forgot to mind what was happening to the plane. Instead, she experienced a feeling of loss when she thought that once they touched ground, the family would disappear and she would lose forever, what the mother herself would offer in explanation for the label.

'Excuse me,' she said, turning to the mother. And the latter also turned to look at her fully.

'Does your daughter also carry a label?'

'You mean the tag?' asked the mother.

'Yes,' said Sissie. 'If you don't mind, may I ask you a rather personal question?'

'Sure,' the mother said, her voice cautious all the same.

'Why have you pinned the labels on the children?'

The mother now gave her full attention to Sissie.

'You mean the t-a-g-s?' she drawled clearly now, like how everyone outside the United States imagines all Americans speak.

'Yes . . . well I was just wondering . . . because this is the first time I've seen anything like it, and . . .'

'Oh, I don't know . . . I don't think I'm the only one doing this sort of thing . . . well, at least I don't hope so . . .'

And Sissie noted with some unhappiness that the woman was anxious, as if she, the mother, felt cross-examined, or accused of being something less than normal. And yet, Sissie didn't know how to put across what she had thought was a genuine curiosity, a plain desire to understand. She wished she could bite her tongue. But the mother was speaking on, anyway . . .

'Well, see, one just never knows what can happen. I've always done it. Since my little girl was a baby. I figured it will make identification easier in case of trouble.'

'Oh . . . oh . . . h . . . yes, of course,' Sissie agreed, while her mind secretly echoed a recognition:

'And air crash victims don't normally offer much as pieces of meat: do they?'

She shivered: though the mother's voice now moved on with a little more confidence.

'Besides, it also helps in terms of who to contact immediately and all that kind of stuff.'

Of course, of course.
The children might get mashed up.
But their labels will be safe from all but fire.

Secure within their plastics which
no hail, no snow, neither war nor pestilence
no water, no blood
can touch.

So what dinosaur ever talked of King Cotton?
All hail Emperor Oil! Step slightly
Nana Black Gold.

We sing the praises of Incorruptible Plastic
the miracle child of a wondrous century.

It appeared the mother still felt a little apologetic: 'Allen and I
have had to live apart most of the time we've been married.
Commuter couple is what they call our type. These things
happen. But whenever we can, we try to be together. Like we
always try to spend our weekends in one place. That means we
fly all the time. Or nearly all the time.'

Sissie didn't think she would ever recover from this piece of
information. Certainly, to fly in and out any distance most
week-ends is definitely to fly all the time . . . So, in what part of
the universe and how many centuries gone past had Sissie envied
the ease with which so many women kept two homes in different
towns, and struggled desperately to bridge the distances with
buses, private or state-owned?

    Kumase – Ga
    Takoradi – Oguaa
    Koo'dua – Keta
    Off Friday afternoon, back Sunday evening.

Then she knew that between her country of origin and her new
environment, the differences were so much in many things and
yet so few in others, the best thing to do might be never to try
to figure anything else out.

'. . . So I was thinking that one ought to put tags on the kids.
I never forget them. At first Allen didn't like the idea a'all. Made
him feel funny, he said. But now, he doesn't mind them, anyhow
it makes me feel better.' The last statement sounded like a
defiance.

149

Hmm, Sweet Sister Courage

There is time. There is time. Time to shop for clothes and food.

Time to answer awkward questions about the moon and the sun and why daddy too can't make the new baby brother, instead of mammy again.

Time to deal with the newest African menace: insulting anonymous telephone calls from the frustrated unmarried sisters your husband is busy chasing.

And here and now, there must be Time to type out tags to label children just in case any old weekend, they might become bits of torn flesh, debris.

Sissie's throat felt like it had been sewn up. It was therefore natural that just when she was realizing that they had not crashed after all, and in fact, they were touching ground smoothly, she should remember too, with infinite humility, those defiled ancestresses who had been shipped across the seas. And she wondered where they had hidden their bowel-begotten infants, rather than leave them to grow up in slavery.

Hei, Hei, Hei

Sweet Sister Courage, hei:

courage to welcome death who bears lives . . .

So what then are two or three years? Isn't absence bearable for those who know ultimate togetherness?

And time does fly so?

Hei, Hei, Hei.

Maybe courage is all, and for the rest,

grief is part of

150

the theatre? and tears are orgasmic?
Dear Mother Courage:
my mother silk.
Hei . . .